D0952506

FOREWORD
BY CHARLES MCGRATH

BACK IN THE 1970S, when all of Joseph Mitchell was out of print, you could, with a little luck, still come across a used copy of *McSorley's Wonderful Saloon* or *The Bottom of the Harbor*. At one point I owned copies of both, but then foolishly lent them to friends, who are presumably still hoarding them, just like whoever it was who walked off with the New York Public Library's sole copy of *Old Mr. Flood*, which today is still listed as "missing." This present edition is the first I've ever set eyes on.

The original *Mr. Flood* is the rarest of rarities, sort of like the mysterious black clams that Mr. Flood, who knows his seafood, is so high on— shellfish so unusual that few people have ever seen them, let alone eaten one. And to extend the analogy in a way that Mitchell, the least metaphorical of writers, never would, the book also resembles the black clam, the *Arctica islandica*, in being the best and most intense of its kind. This shortest of Mitchell's books, barely more than a hundred pages, is also the most Mitchellian, the one that in distilled and concentrated form sums up all the others. If your library were to contain only one Mitchell book, this should be it, and you should probably chain it down.

I first read *Old Mr. Flood* the way most of us lucky enough to work at *The New Yorker* in the '70s and '80s did—in the original three magazine installments, which came out in 1944 and 1945. If you were a young person at the magazine then, reading *Mr. Flood* was a sort of rite of passage. Eventually, if you were lucky enough, some senior figure—Calvin Trillin, perhaps, or Philip Hamburger or William Maxwell—would decide that you weren't completely hopeless, and suggest that you might want to look at some Mitchell.

His work, like that of everyone else who had ever written for *The New Yorker*, was collected in a big black scrapbook, the original magazine columns cut out and pasted, family-album style, on large manila sheets that decades later still smelled of rubber cement. The scrapbooks were shelved alphabetically in the magazine's library, the spines hand-lettered in white ink, and except perhaps for "Salinger, J. D.," I doubt that any was more carefully pored over than "Mitchell, Joseph." The pieces collected there were recognizably *New Yorker*-ish in that they were stylish, meticulous, often surprising and offbeat, but they were also unlike anything else in that entire library. They were in a voice, at once classical and vernacular, that seemed to come out of nowhere (or maybe the part of nowhere that Twain also sprang from) and that none of Mitchell's many admirers have ever come close to imitating. If Mitchell wasn't the single best writer who ever appeared in *The New Yorker*, then it was a tie between him and E. B. White.

What added to the mystery and allure of those scrapbooked Mitchell pieces, and especially of the "stories of fish-eating, whiskey, death, and rebirth" that make up *Old Mr. Flood*, was that the author himself, though he had famously not published for years, came into *The New Yorker*, where he had an office, all the time. A Mitchell sighting was a regular occasion but an exciting one all the same. Joe was formal and courtly: he wore a suit every day—beautiful worsteds in fall and winter; seersucker when the weather was warm—and either a fedora or a straw hat. He was also shy and a little bit secretive. He once began a conversation with me by saying, "Don't tell anyone, but I read something interesting in *The Times* today…"

He was a famously good listener, who would nod his head repeatedly no matter what you told him and say in his soft Tar Heel accent, "Ah know, Ah *know*." But if he felt comfortable and you got him on the right subject, he was also a brilliant and tireless talker. While blotting his head on a hot summer day in a *New Yorker* men's room, he once astonished me by reeling off from memory entire poems by Elizabeth Bishop. On another occasion he explained to me the doctrinal differences between North Carolina Baptists and Methodists with all the zeal of a Zwingli or a Melanchthon. This conversation also took place in the men's room, and I was gone so long somebody came in to look for me. But in my experience his favorite subjects were his beloved "J.J."—James Joyce, that is, whose work he read over and over—and the Fulton Fish Market, the setting, as it happens, of *Old Mr. Flood*, and the place where for some reason Joseph Mitchell, the son of a North Carolina tobacco farmer, may have felt most at home.

Much has been made in recent years of the fact that *Old Mr. Flood* is partly fictional—that, as he wrote in the introduction to the book, "Mr. Flood is not one man" and that these stories, though "solidly based on facts," are "truthful rather than factual." In retrospect, it's hard to understand why people at the time were so surprised. Nowadays, the title and the main character's name are often taken, wrongly, to be an allusion to Edward Arlington Robinson's famous poem "Mr. Flood's Party." (Mitchell later said that at the time of writing he had never read the poem, which makes it one of very few gaps in his literary knowledge.) But Flood is clearly a watery pseudonym nonetheless, and he shares a birthday—July 27—with the author himself. Flood is a composite, Mitchell says, but he is also an alter ego, who has countless things in common with his creator: a love for the fish market, a fondness for a drink every now and then, a habit of collecting stone and iron ornaments from old buildings, a ready ear for a good story, and, most of all, what Mitchell called a "graveyard sense of humor."

Flood, it's not too much to say, is Mitchell as he sometimes imagined himself, truthfully if not altogether factually, and the world of the book is a kind of alternate universe—it's the real, recognizable New York but enhanced a little, so that, for one thing, if you stick, like Mr. Flood, to a sensible diet of whiskey and fish, you really can hope to be a hundred and fifteen years old. The book ends, we should remember, under a full moon, when people, especially "the Irish and the Scandinavians and the people who come up here from the South," get a little larky and delusional. The dream in this case is an almost Shakespearean one, in which life is transformed by the spell of storytelling.

THESE STORIES OF FISH-EATING, whiskey, death, and rebirth first appeared in *The New Yorker*. Mr. Flood is not one man; combined in him are aspects of several old men who work or hang out in Fulton Fish Market, or who did in the past. I wanted these stories to be truthful rather than factual, but they are solidly based on facts. I am obliged to half the people in the market for helping me get these facts. I am much obliged to the following:

Mrs. James Donald, proprietor; James Donald, head bartender; and Gus Trein, manager, of the Hartford House, 309 Pearl Street.

Louis Morino, proprietor of Sloppy Louie's Restaurant, 92 South Street.

Drew Radel, president of the Andrew Radel

Oyster Company, South Norwalk, Connecticut.

The late Amos Chesebro, one of the founders of Chesebro Brothers, Robbins & Graham, Stalls 1, 2, and 3, Fulton Fish Market, and the late Matthew J. Graham, of the same firm. Mr. Chesebro died in December, 1946, lacking a few weeks of reaching the age of ninety-three.

Joe Cantalupo, president of the Cantalupo Carting Company, 140 Beckman Street. Mr. Cantalupo is an antiquarian; he collects prints and photographs of old buildings in the fish-market district and environs. His company, which was founded by his father, Pasquale Cantalupo, sweeps and hoses down the market and carts the market trash—broken barrels and boxes, gurry, and discarded fish—to the city incinerators. His trucks are decorated with this sign:

"A LOAD ON THIS TRUCK

IS A LOAD OFF YOUR MIND."

F. Nelson Blount, president of the Narragansett Bay Packing Company, Warren, Rhode Island. Mr. Blount dredges black clams.

OLD MR. FLOOD

For Jack and Sandra Mitchell

OLD MR. FLOOD

A TOUGH SCOTCH-IRISHMAN I KNOW, Mr. Hugh G. Flood, a retired house-wrecking contractor, aged ninety-three, often tells people that he is dead set and determined to live until the afternoon of July 27, 1965, when he will be a hundred and fifteen years old. "I don't ask much here below," he says. "I just want to hit a hundred and fifteen. That'll hold me." Mr. Flood is small and wizened. His eyes are watchful and icy-blue, and his face is red, bony, and clean-shaven. He is old-fashioned in appearance. As a rule, he wears a high, stiff collar, a candy-striped shirt, a serge suit, and a derby. A silver watch-chain hangs across his vest. He keeps a flower in his lapel. When I am in the Fulton Fish Market neighborhood, I always drop into the Hartford

House, a drowsy waterfront hotel at 309 Pearl Street, where he has a room, to see if he is still alive.

Many aged people reconcile themselves to the certainty of death and become tranquil; Mr. Flood is unreconcilable. There are three reasons for this. First, he deeply enjoys living. Second, he comes of a long line of Baptists and has a nagging fear of the hereafter, complicated by the fact that the descriptions of heaven in the Bible are as forbidding to him as those of hell. "I don't really want to go to either one of those places," he says. He broods about religion and reads a chapter of the Bible practically every day. Even so, he goes to church only on Easter. On that day he has several drinks of Scotch for breakfast and then gets in a cab and goes to a Baptist church in Chelsea. For at least a week thereafter he is gloomy and silent. "I'm a God-fearing man," he says, "and I believe in Jesus Christ crucified, risen, and coming again, but one sermon a year is all I can stand." Third, he is a diet theorist—he calls himself a seafoodetarian—and feels obliged to reach a spectacular age in order to prove his theory. He is convinced that the eating of meat and vegetables shortens life and he maintains that the only sensible food for man, particularly for a man who wants to hit a hundred and fifteen, is fish.

To Mr. Flood, the flesh of finfish and shellfish is not only good to eat, it is an elixir. "When I get through tearing a lobster apart, or one of those tender West Coast octopuses," he says, "I feel like I had a drink from the fountain of youth." He eats with relish every kind of seafood, including sea-urchin eggs, blowfish tails, winkles, ink squids, and barn-door skates. He especially likes an ancient Boston breakfast dish—fried cod tongues, cheeks, and sounds, sounds being the gelatinous air bladders along the cod's backbone. The more unusual a dish, the better he likes it. It makes him feel superior to eat something that most people would edge away from. He insists, however, on the plainest of cooking. In his opinion, there are only four first-class fish restaurants in the city—Sweet's and Libby's on Fulton Street, Gage & Tollner's in Brooklyn, and Lundy's in Sheepshead Bay—and even these, he says, are disinclined to let well enough alone. Consequently, he takes most of his meals in Sloppy Louie Morino's, a busy-bee on South Street frequented almost entirely by wholesale fishmongers from Fulton Market, which is across the street. Customarily, when Mr. Flood is ready for lunch, he goes to the stall of one of the big wholesalers, a friend of his, and browses among the bins for half an hour or so. Finally he picks out a fish, or an eel, or a crab, or the wing of a skate, or whatever looks best that day, buys it, carries it unwrapped to Louie's, and tells the chef precisely how he wants it cooked. Mr. Flood and the chef, a surly old Genoese, are close friends. "I've made quite a study of fish cooks," Mr. Flood says, "and I've decided that old Italians are best. Then comes old colored men, then old mean Yankees, and then old drunk Irishmen. They have to be old; it takes almost a lifetime to learn how to do a thing simply. Even the stove has to be old. If the cook is an awful drunk, so much the better. I don't think a teetotaler could cook a fish. Oh, if he was a mean old tobacco-chewing teetotaler, he might."

Mr. Flood's attitude toward seafood is not altogether mystical. "Fish," he says, "is the only grub left that the scientists haven't been able to get their hands on and improve. The flounder you eat today hasn't got any more damned vitamins in it than the flounder your great-great-granddaddy ate, and it tastes the same. Everything else has been improved *and* improved *and* improved to such an extent that it ain't fit to eat. Consider the egg. When I was a boy on Staten Island, hens ate grit and grasshoppers and scraps from the table and whatever they could scratch out of the ground, and a platter of scrambled eggs was a delight. Then the scientists developed a special egg-laying mash made of old corncobs and sterilized buttermilk, and nowadays you order scrambled eggs and you get a platter of yellow glue. Consider the apple. Years ago you could enjoy an apple. Then the scientists took hold and invented chemical fertilizers especially for apple trees, and apples got big and red and shiny and beautiful and absolutely tasteless. As for vegetables, vegetables have been improved until they're downright poisonous. Two-thirds of the population has the stomach jumps, and no wonder."

Except for bread and butter, sauces, onions, and baked potatoes, Mr. Flood himself has rarely eaten anything but seafood since 1885 and he is in sound shape. For a man past ninety who worked hard in the wet and the wind from boyhood until the age of eighty, he is, in fact, a phenomenon; he has his own teeth, he hears all right, he doesn't wear glasses, his mind seldom wanders, and his appetite is so good that immediately after lunch he begins speculating about what he will have for dinner. He walks cautiously and a little feebly, it is true, but without a stick unless there is snow on the sidewalks. "All I dread is accidents," he said recently. "A broken bone would most likely wind things up for me. Aside from that, I don't fret about my health. I'm immune to the average germ; don't even catch colds; haven't had a cold since 1912. Only reason I caught that one, I went on a toot and it was a pouring-down rainy night in the dead of winter and my shoes were cracked and they let the damp in and I lost my balance a time or two and sloshed around in the gutter and somewhere along the line I mislaid my hat and I'd just had a haircut and I stood in a draft in one saloon an hour or more and there was a poor fellow next to me sneezing his head off and when I got home I crawled into a bed that was beside an open window like a fool and passed out with my wet clothes on, shoes and all.

Also, I'd spent the night before sitting up on a train and hadn't slept a wink and my resistance was low. If the good Lord can just see His way clear to protect me from accidents, no stumbling on the stairs, no hell-fired automobiles bearing down on me in the dark, no broken bones, I'll hit a hundred and fifteen easy."

Mr. Flood doesn't think much of doctors and never goes near one. He passes many evenings in a comfortable old spindle-back chair in the barroom of the Hartford House, drinking Scotch and tap water and arguing, and sometimes late at night he unaccountably switches to brandy and wakes up next morning with an overwhelming hangover—which he calls a katzenjammer. On these occasions he goes over to S. A. Brown's, at 28 Fulton Street, a highly aromatic little drugstore which was opened during President Thomas Jefferson's second term and which specializes in outfitting medicine chests for fishing boats, and buys a bottle of Dr. Brown's Next Morning, a proprietary greatly respected in the fish market. For all other ailments, physical or mental, he eats raw oysters. Once, in the Hartford barroom, a trembly fellow in his seventies, another tenant of the hotel, turned to Mr. Flood and said, "Flood, I had a birthday last week. I'm getting on. I'm not long for this world."

Mr. Flood snorted angrily. "Well, by God, *I* am," he said. "I just got started."

The trembly fellow sighed and said, "I'm all out of whack. I'm going uptown and see my doctor."

Mr. Flood snorted again. "Oh, shut up," he said. "Damn your doctor! I tell you what you do. You get right out of here and go over to Libby's oyster house and tell the man you want to eat some of his big oysters. Don't sit down. Stand up at that fine marble bar they got over there, where you can watch the man knife them open. And tell him you intend to drink the oyster liquor; he'll knife them on the cup shell, so the liquor won't spill. And be sure you get the big ones. Get them so big you'll have to rear back to swallow, the size that most restaurants use for fries and stews; God forgive them, they don't know any better. Ask for Robbins Islands, Mattitucks, Cape Cods, or Saddle Rocks. And don't put any of that red sauce on them, that cocktail sauce, that mess, that gurry. Ask the man for half a lemon, poke it a time or two to free the juice, and squeeze it over the oysters. And the first one he knifes, pick it up and smell it, the way you'd smell a rose, or a shot of brandy. That briny, sea-weedy fragrance will clear your head; it'll make your blood run faster. And don't just eat six; take your time and eat a dozen, eat two dozen, eat three dozen, eat four dozen. And then leave the man a generous tip and go buy yourself a fifty-cent cigar and put your hat on the side of your head and take a walk down to Bowling Green. Look at the sky! Isn't it blue? And look at the girls a-tap-tap-tapping past on their pretty little feet! Aren't they just the finest girls you ever saw, the bounciest, the rump-iest, the laughingest? Aren't you ashamed of yourself for even thinking about spending good money on a damned doctor? And along about here, you better be careful. You're apt to feel so bucked-up you'll slap strangers on the back, or kick a window in, or fight a cop, or jump on the tailboard of a truck and steal a ride."

MR. FLOOD SOLD HIS HOUSE-WRECKING BUSINESS, the H. G. Flood Demolition & Salvage Co., Inc., a prosperous enterprise, in 1930, when he was eighty. A year and a half later, Mrs. Flood, his second wife, died. Directly after the funeral he gave up his apartment in Chelsea, put his furniture in storage, and moved into the Hartford, a hotel he had known and admired for many years as a truly peaceful place. "I was sadly in need of peace and quiet when I moved into here," he once said. "I had a saintly wife, God rest her. She was opposed to anything and everything in the line of fun. Use to, when I showed up with a load on, she'd persecute me. She never offered to hit me. She just stood in the door with her head thrown back and howled. She used both lungs and it didn't seem possible for all that racket to come out of one human mouth. Some nights I was afraid my eardrums wouldn't stand the strain. Once I said to her, 'Mary, dear, I'm thankful to God you ain't a drinking woman. If you can make that much noise cold sober, just think what you could do on a little gin.'"

The Hartford stands on the southwest corner of the junction of Pearl Street, Ferry Street, and Peck Slip, down in the old city. The South Ferry branch of the Third Avenue elevated line goes past it, on

Pearl Street. The fish market is a couple of blocks to the south of it, and The Swamp, the tannery district, is one block north. Rooms run from three-fifty to four-fifty a week. Mr. Flood took one of the four-fifty rooms, and he has been happy in it. "You take an old retired widower crock like me," he says, "the perfect place for him is some back-alley hotel where he can be among his own kind, the rough element. I've got a married daughter by my first wife, and she begged me to go live with her. Praise the Lord I didn't! Like I said to her, 'Louise, in a month you'd hate the sight of me, and vice versa. You couldn't help it. That's nature. You'd be wanting me to die and get out of the way, and I'd probably go ahead and die, just to be accommodating.'" Mr. Flood is well off and could undoubtedly afford the Waldorf-Astoria, but newness depresses him. Like most old people, he feels best when he is around things that have lasted a long time. The Hartford is the oldest hotel in continuous operation in the city, and it just suits him. It was opened in 1836 as the Eastern Pearl Street House; the name was changed in the late sixties, when steamboats from Hartford and other New

England ports docked nearby in Peck Slip. It is a shoebox-shaped building of five stories, it is surrounded by factories and hide and spice warehouses, and at night the friendly light in its combined lobby, barroom, and dining room is the only light that can be seen for blocks around. A flower-basket design is cut in the thick glass of the front door, across from the bar is a row of rickety spindle-backs, the bill of fare is scribbled in chalk on a big slate on the dining-room wall, and at the foot of the stairs is an oak rack on which the tenants hook their keys when they come down in the morning. The keys are heavy and each is attached to a serrated brass fob nearly the size of a saucer. There is no elevator. On the back-bar shelf are several photographs of the hotel. One, taken in 1901, shows Buffalo Bill and some Indians in fringed buckskins eating lobsters at a family table in the dining room. Around the margin, in a crabbed hand, someone has written, "Col. Buffalo Bill and 1 doz. red Indians just off the Boston boat, stayed three days, big eaters, lobster every meal, up all night, took the place."

The Hartford has about forty-five tenants right

now, most of them elderly mariners who have retired on savings or pensions. Some of them do not budge out of the place, even to take a turn around the block, for weeks on end. Six were merchant-ship officers, four were Hudson River bargemen, two worked on scallop dredges, one owned a pair of harbor tugs, one operated three rows of shad nets in the Hudson off Edgewater, New Jersey, one had a bait barge in Sheepshead Bay, and one was captain of a seiner in the old Long Island Sound gurry-fleet that caught moss-bunkers for fertilizer factories. A few are grim and withdrawn and still unused to idleness after years of it. These stay quietly in their rooms much of the time. About a dozen are beery and wildly imaginative mythomaniacs, and Mr. Flood is often in their company. These get up at dawn, bustle downstairs to the barroom, and start talking big during breakfast; at closing time, around midnight, they are still there and still talking big. Before the night bartender goes home, he usually has to help two or three up the stairs and put them to bed; he considers this one of his duties. Some are cranks, but the proprietor, Mrs. James Donald, does not mind that. She says she has noticed that day in and day out it is easier to do business with a cranky man than with one who has forever got a grin on his face. Mrs. Donald is a handsome, friendly woman of Huguenot and German ancestry. She inherited the Hartford from her first husband, Diedrich Bloete, who had owned it since 1901. A brother of hers, Gus Trein, is manager. Her present husband, a retired policeman, is head bartender.

Mr. Flood's room is on the top floor. Its furnishings remind him pleasantly of years gone by; there is a brass bed, a washstand with pitcher and bowl, a wicker rocking chair, and a marble-top table. "The furniture in here goes back about as far as I do," he said one day. He has decorated one wall with a set of cardboard posters designed for display in retail fish stores, which he picked up in the office of the Fishery Council, the market's chamber of commerce. Among them are the following:

CRABS FROM THE BAY

ARE A TREAT ANY DAY.

FRESH MACKEREL IS IN SEASON

AT A COST WITHIN REASON.

BE OF GOOD CHEER

OYSTERS R HERE.

On another wall, just above the head of the bed, Mr. Flood has tacked up a map of Staten Island. He was born there. Once I asked him a question about his youth. He frowned and said, "My boy, I like to talk, but I don't much like to talk about my past. It's a sure sign of second childhood." On another occasion, however, he said, "I'm a third-generation Staten Islander. I'm from Pleasant Plains, a village on the south shore. My grandfather and my father before me were carpenters. I had an uncle in Brooklyn who was a general contractor—dwellings and small factories—and I went to work for him when I was a boy. Let me give you some advice: never work for your own flesh and blood. My uncle was a big-hearted man. Once I saw him chip in with a five-dollar bill to assist the family of a poor fellow who had been his bookkeeper for thirty-five years and died without funeral money. I worked for him I think it was sixteen years and then I got wise to myself and quit and became a house-wrecking contractor. I think I got into that line out of spite."

Mr. Flood's room has one window, and from it,

looking south, he can see the gilded bluefish on the weathervane atop the great gray shed of the Fulton Market Fishmongers Association, a sight of which he is fond. Mr. Flood is tidy about his person; he goes to the barber every day, he keeps his suits pressed, and his derby is seldom dusty. His room, however, is extraordinarily untidy. He rarely lets the maid clean it. Above the washstand hangs a water-splotched calendar for 1932 on which the month pad, even the leaf for January, is still intact. On the marble-top table are four grape baskets filled with sea shells and river shells. He is a shell collector. One of his most prized possessions is a group of fresh-water mussel shells. They were given to him by a dealer in live carp in Peck Slip who got them, on a buying trip, from some Tennessee River carp fishermen who dredge mussels for the pearl-button trade as a sideline. Mr. Flood has shells of nine species. Each has, in addition to its Latin name, a name that is used in the trade. "I've got a pig toe, a pistol grip, a heel splitter, a warty back, a maple leaf, a monkey face, a rose bud, a rabbit's foot, and a but-terfly," he says with pride. "I *had* a washboard, a lady finger, and a mule ear, but I came home one night in poor order and I was reeling around and I couldn't find the light cord and they were on the floor and I stepped on them." The floor around Mr. Flood's rocking chair is always cluttered. Scattered every which way about it the last time I visited him were a wooden shrimp scoop that he knocks his cigar ashes into, a kind of fish knife known as a ripper, a whiskbroom, a Bible, two volumes of Mark Twain (he owns a ten-volume, large-type set), a scrapbook filled with yellowing clippings of Heywood Broun's column in the *World-Telegram*, a copy of the *War Cry*, the magazine that Salvation Army women hawk on street corners, and an old, beautifully written United States Bureau of Fisheries reference book, "Fishes of the Gulf of Maine," which he ordered years ago from the Government Printing Office and which he reads over and over. He knows the habits and ranges of hundreds of fishes, mollusks, and crustaceans; he has even memorized the Latin names of many of them. Twain and Broun are Mr. Flood's favorite writers. "If I get to heaven," he once said, "the first Saturday night I'm up there, if it's O.K. with the management, I'm going to get hold of a bottle of good whiskey and look up Mr. Twain and Mr. Broun. And if they're not up there, I'll ask to be sent down to the other place." A moment later he added uneasily, "Of course, I don't really mean that. I'm just talking to hear myself talk."

Mr. Flood visits the fish market every weekday morning. He rises at five, has a cup of black coffee in the Hartford dining room, lights a cigar, and begins a leisurely tour of the fish stalls, the oyster sheds, the flounder-filleting houses, the smoking lofts, and the piers. When he reaches Fulton Street, the pandemonium in the market invigorates him. He throws his shoulders back, sniffs the salty air, and rubs his palms together. To him, the reek of the fish houses is not unpleasant. "I'll tell you a valuable secret," he once said. "The Fulton Fish Market smell will cure a cold within twenty minutes. Nobody that works in the market ever has a cold. They don't know what a cold is. The fishmongers are afraid the general public will find this out. It's too crowded around here as it is, and if the public took to coming down here to cure their colds there wouldn't be room enough to turn around in." When making his tour, he dresses like a boss fishmonger, wearing a full-length white apron and knee-high rubber boots. The streets down there, as well as the floors of the stalls, are constantly being hosed down, and he believes in heeding the old market proverb, "Keep your feet dry and you'll never die." He goes first to the piers and looks on as the trawlers, draggers, and scallop dredges are unloaded. The fishermen treat him with respect and answer all his questions. They seem to think that he is an official of some kind. The call him Pop or Commissioner. One morning I was standing on the Fulton Street pier with Edmond Irwin, supervisor of the Fishery Council, when Mr. Flood came poking along. He looked down into an unloading trawler from New Bedford and yelled, "Hey, Captain, step over here!" The captain stopped what he was doing, obediently crossed his deck, and peered up at Mr. Flood, who asked, "What you got today, Captain?"

"Nothing to speak of, sir," the captain said. "Just a load of flounders—blackbacks and yellowtails."

"Fine, fine, Captain," said Mr. Flood. "You got enough filly of sole in that load for five thousand dinners. Where'd you go this trip?"

"We was up north of Brown's Bank."

"Up in The Gully?"

"That's right. We was up in The Gully."

"Fine, fine, Captain!" said Mr. Flood, beaming and rubbing his hands. "That's just fine!"

Mr. Flood moved on down the pier. The captain stared after him for a moment, obviously puzzled, and then turned to Mr. Irwin and said, "Ed, who in hell is that man, anyway? Does he work for the government, or what?"

"It's hard to say," Mr. Irwin said. "All I know he's an old boy who's trying to live to be a hundred and fifteen years old by eating fish."

"God bless us!" said the captain. "How far along is he?"

"He's way past ninety," Mr. Irwin said.

"I declare to Jesus!" the captain said. "Well, we live and learn. Maybe I ought to start eating fish."

After Mr. Flood has inspected the boats, he goes into the shed of the Fishmongers Association. He listens to the blasphemous haggling between the fishmongers and the buyers from the retail fish stores, asks scores of questions, peers into bins, hefts and admires a striped bass here and a red snapper there, and carries market gossip from one stall to the next. He has so much curiosity that a few of the fishmongers look the other way when they see him coming, but the others treat him considerately and sometimes introduce him to visitors as the Mayor of the Fish Market. Presently he leaves the shed and steps into one of the filleting houses on South Street and helps himself to a bucket of gurry, or fish scraps, with which to feed some one-legged gulls that he has adopted. The fish market supports a flock of several hundred gulls and there are always a few crippled ones among them. "This condition," Mr. Flood says, "is due to the fact that sea gulls don't understand traffic lights. There's a stretch of South Street running through the market that's paved with Belgian blocks. And every so often during the morning rush a fish or two and sometimes a whole slew of them drop off a truck and are ground up by the wheels and packed down tight into the cracks between the blocks. The gulls go wild when they see this. They wait until traffic gets halted by a red light, and then they drop out of the sky like bats out of hell and try to worry the fish from between the cracks with their beaks and

claws. They're stubborn birds. They get so inter-
ested they don't notice when the light changes and
all of a sudden, wham bang, the heavy truck traffic
is right on top of them. Some get killed outright.
Some get broken wings and flop off and hide
somewhere and starve to death. Those that lose
only one leg are able to keep going, but the other
gulls peck them and claw them and treat them as
outcasts and they have a hard, hard time." The
crippled gulls are extremely distrustful, but Mr.
Flood has been able to make friends with a few of
them. When he strides onto a pier toting a bucket of
gurry they circle down and surround him. One or
two will eat from his hands.

Mr. Flood finishes feeding his gulls around
nine o'clock. Then he is ready for his first drink of
the day. He is opposed to drinking alone—he says
it leads to the mumbles—so he proceeds along
South Street, hunting for company. He often goes
to the freshwater branch of the market, in Peck Slip,
and invites Mrs. Birdy Treppel, a veteran fishwife,
to step into a bar and grill near her stand and have
one. "I *do* need a little something," she usually says,
"to thaw me out." Mr. Flood and Mrs. Treppel are

old friends. She fascinates him because she is always cold. Mrs. Treppel handles a variety of fresh-water fish, including carp, whitefish, pike, buffaloes, and red horses, and her stand, a three-bin affair partly on the sidewalk under a tarpaulin shelter and partly in the gutter, is in Peck Slip, just below Water Street, right in the path of the wind from the harbor. "I am beautifully situated," she says, "on the corner of Influenza Street and Pneumonia Slip." In the wintertime, Mrs. Treppel lets an assistant handle the bulk of her trade, while she keeps a fire jumping in an old oil drum beside her stand, feeding it with barrel staves and discarded fish boxes. She says that it doesn't do much good. She hovers near the fire, shivering, with her arms in her apron, which she rolls up and uses as a muff. She has a nervous habit of hopping up and down and stamping her feet. She does this in the heat of the summer as well as in the winter; she can't seem to stop. She appears to be unusually corpulent, but she says that this is misleading. "I'm really a thin little thing, nothing but skin and bones," she says, "but I got on twelve layers of clothes—thirteen, counting my shimmy. If you was to see me undressed you wouldn't know me." One morning I was going through the market with Mr. Flood. We paused beside Mrs. Treppel's fire and he said, "Birdy, tell the man how cold it gets in Peck Slip." "Well, son, I tell you," she said, hopping up and down as she talked, "if you went up to the North Pole in the dead of December and stripped to the drawers and picked out the biggest iceberg up there and dug a hole right down to the heart of it and crawled in that hole and put a handful of snow under each arm and sat on a block of ice and et a dish of ice cream, why, you wouldn't be nowhere near as cold as you'd be in Peck Slip in a sheepskin coat with a box fire in the gutter."

Another fish-market notable with whom Mr. Flood occasionally takes a first-today drink is Mr. Ah Got Um, a high-spirited Savannah Negro who operates a retail fish store on Lenox Avenue in Harlem and who attends the market two mornings a week to do his buying. If he feels good, he chants as he walks through the stalls:

> *Ah got pompanos!*
> *Ah got buffaloes!*
> *Ah got these!*
> *Ah got those!*

Ah got um!

Ah got um!

Ah'm the ah-got-um man!

Around eleven o'clock, Mr. Flood shows up for lunch at Sloppy Louie's. The last time I visited him, we had lunch together. He had decided on a blue-black sea bass that day, and while the chef was broiling it we sat at a table up front, talking. A young fishmonger in an Army uniform, on furlough and looking up his colleagues in the market, came in. Mr. Flood hadn't seen him in a year or so. "Why, hello, Pop," the soldier said. "Are *you* still alive?" Mr. Flood's face fell. "Look here, son," he said. "That's a rather personal question." He became gloomy and didn't say anything for a while. When the chef brought his fish in, however, he started talking again. "You're damned right I'm still alive," he said, opening his fish and deftly removing its spine and fin bones. "Fact of the matter is, I feel the best I've felt in years. I et four dozen oysters last night and I felt so good I almost had an oyster fit." He stared at me for a moment. "Did you ever see anybody have an oyster fit?" he asked.

"No, sir," I said.

"My boy," Mr. Flood said, "people who are unaccustomed to oysters sometimes behave real queer after putting away a few dozen. I've witnessed many seizures of this nature. I'll tell you about one. My daughter Louise lives up in South Norwalk, Connecticut, and I visit her once a year, the first week in September, when the oysters come back in season. I've got a good friend in South Norwalk, Mr. Drew Radel, president of the Andrew Radel Oyster Company. Drew owns twenty-two thousand acres of oyster beds in the Sound and he produces the biggest oyster in the United States, the Robbins Island. Some get as big as omelettes. His main dock is located on the Norwalk River, and when I'm visiting my daughter I walk down there every day and Drew and I sit around and talk and eat oysters.

"Well, back in September, 1934, during the depression, Drew and I were on the dock, talking, and up walked three fellows said they were from Brooklyn. They took off their hats and asked for deckhand jobs on one of Drew's dredge boats. They were weevily fellows, pale, stoop-shouldered, and clerky-looking, three runts, no life in them at all. I don't believe a one of them had cracked a smile in months. Drew took pity on them and hired them. And before they went out to bring in a load of oysters, he took the captain aside and told him to let those Brooklyn boys eat all the oysters they could hold as soon as the dredge got out on the beds. 'Let them stuff themselves,' Drew said. 'It might possibly put some life into them.'

"Well, when the dredge came back the first time, I noticed that those Brooklyn boys were whistling. When it came back the second time, I noticed that they were singing. Late in the afternoon, Drew and I were sitting in his office on the dock when the dredge came back the third time. Shortly after it tied up, I heard a hullabaloo on the dock and I went to the window. Those Brooklyn boys were laughing and shouting and wrestling and throwing each other's hats in the water. They were flinging themselves head over heels. The air was full of Brooklyn boys. One picked up a tin bucket and began to bang on it with a stick—a-rumpatiddy-rumpatiddy-rump-a-tump. He marched up the dock, drumming on the bucket and yodeling, stepping high, a regular one-man band. Another one turned a double somerset and stood on his head right on the edge of the dock. He got up, shook himself, and began to sing a song called 'Tiptoe Through the Tulips with Me.' 'Uh-oh!' I said to Drew. 'The oysters have caught up with them.'

"In a little while they came trooping into Drew's office, whistling. Drew was dictating an important letter and he frowned at them. 'Boys,' he said, 'what in the hell do you want here?' One of them, the littlest, snickered and said, 'We want to throw you off the dock.' 'At the present moment,' Drew said, 'I'm far too busy. You'll have to excuse me.' 'Well, then,' this fellow said, 'we'll box you.' Drew told them he didn't have time right then to do any boxing, and this fellow said, 'In that case, we'll go up the street and find somebody else to box. Will that be all right?' 'Why, yes indeed,' Drew said, 'that'll be all right.' In about half an hour the phone rang and I answered it. It was the sergeant at the police station in South Norwalk, and he said he'd just locked up two men who claimed they worked for the Radel Company. 'That's funny,' I said. 'There should be three of them.' 'Hold the phone a minute,' the sergeant said. 'There's a dreadful racket out in the street.' I held the phone and presently the sergeant came back. 'Everything's O.K.,' he said. 'They're bringing the third man in now, and it's taking four patrolmen, three detectives, and a couple of civilians to do it.'"

Mr. Flood cackled. "Drew and I were so proud of those Brooklyn boys," he said, "we went right over and bailed them out." —*(1944)*

THE BLACK CLAMS

ONE NOVEMBER MORNING I got a letter from Mr. Flood, inviting me to come down to the Hartford House and help him eat a bushel of black clams. "Hope this finds you well and enjoying life to the full," he wrote. "I am well, can't complain. On Friday the next I'll have something down here I want to show you, something highly unusual in the eating line, a bushel of black clams, the mysterious *Arctica islandica*. It's also known as the ocean, or deep-sea, quahog. I doubt you ever even heard of the beast. Until here lately only a few people in the world had seen one, let alone eaten one. Now and then a fisherman would find a nest of empty black clam shells in the belly of a cod or a haddock (these fishes root them off the bottom of the ocean and swallow them whole and naturally the shells don't digest), and every year or so along certain stretches of the New England coast a hurricane or a freaky storm with an onshore wind would tear a small quantity off the bottom somewhere and wash them ashore. A few would be undamaged, and people who picked these up and ate them always spoke highly of their flavor, better than bay quahogs, or steamers, or skimmers, or razor-shells, better than cockles, or winkles, or scallops, or whelks, better than mussels, better than most oysters you get nowadays. All up and down the coast from Boston to Sheepshead Bay the oystermen and clammers tried their best for generations to find out where the black clams come from. They dredged here and they dredged there, but they couldn't locate a bed anywhere at all. It was one of the secrets of the old briny. Now at last they have succeeded. In fact, they have succeeded beyond their wildest dreams. They have just discovered thirteen beds out in the open ocean off Point Judith, Rhode Island. As far as the financial end is concerned, it is like they brought in an oil well. The beds are whoppers. One bed is about as big as R.I. itself, tons of clams, mountains of clams, millions upon millions, untold boatloads, a bellyful of clams for EVERYBODY, glory be to God. One of the fishmongers down here got hold of some last week and we ate them on the half shell. No fault to find. A friend of mine in Warren, R.I., is going to get me a bushel of them on Thursday the next and put them on The Round-Up, the fish train that the N.Y., New Haven & H. runs down five nights a week from Boston. I will pick them up in the market Friday A.M. Come down around noon and meet me in the lobby of the H. H. and we will eat some clams and drink some whiskey and tell some lies and sing the One-eyed Riley. I remain, yrs. very truly, H. G. Flood."

I wrote Mr. Flood that I would meet him at noon on Friday. I showed up in the combined lobby, barroom, and dining room of the Hartford exactly at noon on that day, but he wasn't around. Three of the old men who live in the hotel were sitting on stools at one end of the bar. They had a map spread out and they were hunched over it, each with pencil, probably dividing up Europe to suit themselves. I knew one of them, to speak to, Mr. P. J. Mooney, who used to be part owner of a pair of big harbor tugs, the *Nora T.* and the *Linda Lane.* He is a raucous old man with mournful eyes and a paunch so enormous that he says it embarrasses him. (Mr. Flood once told me that Mr. Mooney, who is a wrestling fan, has a recurring nightmare in which he becomes separated from his paunch, which assumes the shape of a headless wrestler and advances on him. They square off and then they lunge at each other and wrestle for what seems like hours to Mr. Mooney. "Some nights the paunch throws P. J.," Mr. Flood said, "and some nights P. J. throws the paunch. I told P. J. he had a gold mine there. 'Put that match on in Madison Square Garden,' I said to him, 'and you'll go down in history, the both of you. Anyway,' I said, 'you shouldn't fret so much about that paunch. In days to come, when you're too old and feeble to get about at all, it'll keep you company.'") Gus Trein, the manager of the Hartford, was behind the bar, spelling the regular bartender, and he beckoned for me to come over. He seemed worried.

"Mr. Flood telephoned just now," Mr. Trein said, "and asked me to tell you to step over to Tom Maggiani's, the ship chandler on Dover Street. He's waiting for you over there. What in the world is he up to now?"

"All I know," I said, "he invited me to come down and eat some black clams."

Mr. Trein looked at me suspiciously. "Some what did you say?" he asked.

"Some black clams," I said. "They discovered some black clams up in Rhode Island, and Mr. Flood ordered a bushel."

Mr. Trein glanced knowingly at Mr. Mooney and said, "Did you hear that, P. J.?" Mr. Mooney nodded, and then he tapped his forehead with his index finger and described a circle in the air. I became uneasy. "How *is* Mr. Flood?" I asked.

Mr. Trein frowned. "To tell you the God's green truth," he said, "I'm worried about him. He acted real peculiar this morning, didn't he, P. J.?"

"He did," said Mr. Mooney. "He did, indeed. Black clams, be Jesus! That's another delusion. The old boy's out of his head, no doubt about it. When he came downstairs this morning, I was sitting over there reading the paper and I said to him, 'Good morning, Old Man Flood. How you feeling? You look a bit pale.' And he stood and stared at me like he didn't recognize me, like he was deathly afraid of me, and he shouted out, 'Shut up, Old Scratch!' Then he commenced to stomp around the lobby and shake his fist and carry on. 'You got to put a stop to it!' he yelled. 'Coffins! Undertakers! Hearses! Funeral parlors! Cemeteries! Woodlawn! Cypress Hills! Fresh Pond Crematory! Calvary! Green-Wood! It starts the day off wrong! It's more than one man can stand!' That's what he yelled, word for word. Then he got ahold of himself and his mind quit wandering and he looked me straight in the eye and cursed me for a damned old pot-gutted fool. 'I'd be much obliged if you'd keep your trap shut when I come down in the morning, P. J.,' he said to me, 'you damned old pot-gutted fool.' Then he walked about eight or nine feet out of his way and deliberately kicked a chair. I started to inquire what in hell was the matter, but he stomped right past me and went out the side door, mumbling to himself."

"Oh, well," said Mr. Trein, "he just probably got up on the wrong side. Either that or a hangover."

Mr. Mooney snorted. "No, no, no, Gus," he said. "I hate to say this, but Old Man Flood's not long for this world. It's his time to go. I've had my eye on him lately. He's failing, the poor man. He's failing fast. He'll drop off any day now."

I was taken aback by this conversation. I decided that Mr. Flood's gnawing fear of the hereafter had got the best of him and I made up my mind, with misgivings, that I would try to persuade him to go with me and have a talk with a doctor I know at Beekman Hospital, which is at Beekman and Water, on the rim of the fish-market district. I said goodbye to Mr. Trein and Mr. Mooney and started over to Maggiani's. I was quite depressed.

MAGGIANI'S IS A FISHING-BOAT chandlery. There are sixteen boats—ground-fish draggers and trawlers and sea-scallop dredges—that regularly make ten-day voyages from the Fulton Market piers to the banks in the Gulf of Maine, and Maggiani's "grubs" seven of them; that is, it equips them with meat, groceries, and galley gear. The fishermen, most of whom are Scandinavians or Newfoundlanders, are clannish; they don't mix much with the fishmongers and Maggiani's is their favorite hangout in the

market. It is also one of Mr. Flood's favorite hang-
outs. He sometimes behaves as if Maggiani had him
on the payroll; he frequently answers the telephone
and on busy days he pitches in and helps make up
orders. It is hidden away in the rear half of the
ground floor of a converted Revolutionary-period
dwelling on Dover Street, a crooked alley that runs
beneath the Brooklyn Bridge from Franklin Square
to the river. This building is of a type that old-time
Manhattan real-estate men call a humpback; it is
box-square and three stories high, its tar-papered
roof is as steep as an inverted V, it is made of
salmon-colored bricks, and it looks proud and
noble, ten time nobler than the Chrysler Building.
There are several fine humpbacks in the market, a
district that contains the oldest and the most
patched-up commercial buildings in the city. Maggiani's is poorly illuminated, it is as cool as a cellar
in summer and as warm as a kitchen in winter, it
smells garlicky, and it is a pleasant place in which to
sit and doze. Up front, surrounded by a collection
of slat-back chairs and up-ended boxes, is an
oblong coal stove with a cooking hob on it. Nearby
is a deal table on which are some packs of cards, an

accumulation of back numbers of the *Fishing Gazette*, and a greasy *World Almanac*, edition of 1936. There is a big brass spittoon. There is a cat hole in the door, and there are usually two or three burly fish-house cats roving about. Hanging on the walls are a lithograph of Franklin D. Roosevelt, a rusty swordfish harpoon, a photograph of the officers of the Fisherman's Union of the Atlantic, a finger-smudged Coast and Geodetic chart of the Nantucket Shoals, an oar with a mermaid crudely carved on the blade, and a sign which says, "LAUGH AND THE WORLD LAUGHS WITH YOU, WEEP AND YOU WEEP ALONE." In the middle of the tile floor, resting on its side and dominating the room, is a hogshead of molasses with "EXTRA FANCY BARBADOS" stencilled on the spigot end; fishing-boat cooks take along several gallons of high-grade molasses every voyage for flap-jacks and for beans and brown bread. On the days the boats are in, Maggiani's is packed. On such days, Tommaso Maggiani, the proprietor, a Palermitano, puts complimentary platters of cheese, sliced onions, and salami under fly screens on the counter, and he keeps a pot of coffee on the hob, and the loafing fishermen get up from their seats around the stove, yawn, and fix themselves snacks—what they call "mug-ups"—whenever the spirit moves them.

Mr. Flood was in Maggiani's, standing with his back to the stove. He and Mr. Maggiani, who was snoring in a swivel chair with his heels on his roll-top desk, were the only people in the place. As soon as I got a good look at Mr. Flood, I felt relieved. His eyes were alert, his face was ruddy, his shoulders were erect, he was smoking a big cigar, and he shook hands vigorously. As usual, like a boss fishmonger, he had on rubber boots and a stiff straw hat with holes cut in it, and over his blue serge suit he wore a full-length white apron. He had two loaves of Italian bread, wrapped in a piece of newspaper, under his left arm. I asked him how he felt.

"Well," he said, "there are days when I hate everybody in the world, fat, lean, and in between, and this started out to be one of those days, but I had a drop to drink, and now I love everybody."

"Yes," I said, "they told me up at the Hartford you didn't feel so good this morning."

Mr. Flood gave me a sharp look. "Were you talking to P. J. Mooney?" he asked.

"Yes," I said, "I was."

"I thought I could detect the track of his tongue," said Mr. Flood. "What did he tell you?"

"He seemed worried about you."

"What in hell did he tell you?"

"For one thing," I said, "he believes those black clams you wrote about are a delusion. They're not, are they?"

"Are you trying to insult me? What else did he tell you?"

"He said you were failing fast and that he expects you to drop off any day."

Mr. Flood snickered. "Oh, he does, does he?" he said. "Oh, the fat old fool, the miserable, bilious old pot-gutted fool! He got my back up this morning. That's why I brought my clams into here. If I took them up to the Hartford, like I planned, I'd be obliged to offer him some. I used to have a high regard for P. J. Mooney; knows quite a bit about striped-bass fishing, but he's picked up a habit that's so queer—well, it's so queer, so ghouly, so disgusting, so low-down nasty that I don't even like to talk about it. I'll tell you about it later. Here, my boy, have a cigar." He handed me a cigar. It was a

Bulldog Avenue, a perfecto cigar hand-rolled in Tampa that costs sixty-five cents apiece; he buys them by the box. He tossed his two loaves on the counter and went into Maggiani's coldroom, a cubicle in back in which sides of beef are hung to age. In a few moments he came shuffling out with a bushel basket in his arms. The basket was heaped with little pitch-black clams. Grunting, he set it on the counter and tipped it and let about half the contents pour out, cornucopia fashion—an exuberance of clams. The noise awakened Mr. Maggiani, who shouted, "Stop! Stop! Don't you mess up my counter. I just laid new oilcloth on that counter." "Shut up, Tommy," said Mr. Flood, "and go back to sleep."

He strewed about two yards of the counter with clams, and then stepped back and looked at them gloatingly. They were so black they glinted, they were so plump they were almost globular, and they were beautiful. The lips of the shells were tightly shut, a sign of health and freshness—a clam out of water stays shut until it begins to die, and then the adductors, the two muscles that hold the shells together, relinquish their grip and the lips gape. In

Fulton Market and on the Boston Fish Pier, quahogs are graded in three sizes—Little Necks,
cherrystones, and chowders. These black quahogs
were Little Necks, about an inch and three quarters
from hinge to lip, and they were as uniform as silver
dollars. Mr. Flood got out a knife he carries in a belt
holster, a kind of fish knife known as a gut-blade,
and shucked a clam for me. The meat was a rosy
yellow, a lovely color, the color of the flesh next to
the stone of a freestone peach. Bay quahogs have
splotches of yellow in some seasons, but, with the
exception of the liver and the siphons, all of this
clam was yellow—the foot, the muscles, the gills,
the intestines, even the mantle. I ate the clam and
found that it was as tender and sweet-meated as a
Little Neck out of Great South Bay, the finest bay
clam on the whole coast. Then I drank the juice
from the cup of the shell. It was rich, invigorating,
and free of grit, but, surprisingly, not as briny as the
juice of a bay quahog; that was the only fault I
could find with the *Arctica islandica*.

Mr. Maggiani came over with a tray on which
he had put three tumblers, a carafe of water, and a
fifth of Scotch about half full. "Clams don't agree

with me," he said, "but I think I'll eat six or seven dozen, just to be sociable." "Help yourself, Tommy," said Mr. Flood. "That's what they're here for." Mr. Maggiani fixed us each a drink. He poured an extra gollop in Mr. Flood's tumbler and Mr. Flood smiled. "Old age hasn't taught me a whole lot," he said, "but it's sure taught me the true value of a dollar, a kind word, and a drink of whiskey." We had our drinks. Mr. Flood took six lemons and six limes from the pockets of his apron and halved them with his gut-blade to squeeze on the clams. Then he began slicing one of the Italian loaves. Mr. Flood will not eat factory-made American bread; he calls it gurry, a word applied by fishmongers to the waste that is left after a fish has been dressed. "I doubt a hog would eat it," he says, "unless it was toasted and buttered and marmalade put on it and him about to perish to death." Every other morning Mr. Flood walks up to Mrs. Palumbo's *panetteria italiana*, a hole-in-the-wall bakery on Elizabeth Street, and buys a couple of loaves. He takes his meals in restaurants in the fish-market district— Sloppy Louie's, the Hartford dining room, Sweet's, and Libby's—and he always brings his own bread.

Like most Sicilian neighborhood bakers, Mrs. Palumbo turns out loaves in a multitude of shapes, some of which are symbols that protect against the Evil Eye. The loaves that Mr. Flood had this day were long and whole-wheat and S-shaped and decorated with gashes.

Mr. Maggiani, watching Mr. Flood slice, said, "Hugh, do you know the name of that loaf?"

"I heard it once," Mr. Flood said, "but it's slipped my mind."

"It's called a *cosa minuta a zighizaghi*, a small thing with zigzags," Mr. Maggiani said. "The S stands for *sapienza*—wisdom."

Mr. Flood grunted, "Whatever to hell it's called," he said, "it's good. Mrs. Palumbo knows what she's doing. She don't take ads in the papers to tell big black lies about her vitamins, she don't have a radio program rooting and tooting about her enriched bread, she don't wrap in cellophane, she don't even have a telephone. She just goes ahead and bakes the way her great-great-granddaddy baked. Consequently, by God, lo and behold, her bread is fit to eat. I'm not against vitamins, whatever to hell they are, but God took care of that matter away back there in the hitherto—God and nature, and not some big scientist or other. Years back, bread was the staff of life. It looked good, it smelled good, it tasted good, and it had all the vitamins in it a man could stand. Then the bakers fiddled and fooled and improved their methods and got things down to such a fine point that a loaf of bread didn't have any more nourishment in it than a brickbat. Now they're putting the vitamins back in by scientific means—the way God did it don't suit them; it ain't complicated enough—and they've got the brass to get on the radio and brag about it; they should hide their heads in shame."

Mr. Maggiani hadn't been paying much attention to Mr. Flood's remarks; he only half listens to him. Now he pursed his lips and nodded his head a couple of times. "Science is a great thing," he said piously. "It's wonderful what they can do." Mr. Flood stared at him for a moment and then let the matter drop. We had another round of Scotch. Mr. Maggiani found a knife for me and one for himself, and the three of us got down to work on the clams.

"The bed this basket of clams came out of is called Bed Number Two," said Mr. Flood. He is one of those who can talk and eat at once. "It's located two and an eighth miles east-southeast of the whistling buoy off Point Judith, Rhode Island. The water out there is eighty to a hundred and twenty feet deep. That's why it took so long to find the blackies. The bottom of Number Two is muddy, what the Coast and Geodetic charts call sticky, and it's just about solid with clams. They're as thick as germs. Bay clams come from much shallower water. To give you an idea, the water over most of the quahog beds in Great South Bay is only twelve feet deep. The Rhode Island clammers are working the ocean beds with the same kind of dredge boats that oystermen use, except the cables are longer. They lower a dredge on a steel cable and drag it over the bottom. The dredge plows up the mud and the clams are thrown into a big chain-metal bag that's hung on the tail of the dredge. They drag for fifteen minutes, and then they haul up and unload the bag on the deck. The ocean clammers are making a ton of money. They're getting a dollar to a dollar and a half a bushel."

"That don't sound so good," said Mr. Maggiani. "The last I heard, bay clammers were getting two and a half to three."

"A dredge boat can take fifty bushels of bay clams a day," Mr. Flood said, "if the crew don't mind rupturing themselves. The same boat can take two hundred and fifty bushels of blackies a day and just coast along. That's the difference. I heard about one boat that took five hundred and thirty-eight bushels in six hours. Also, most of the beds are outside the three-mile limit and there's no restrictions on the length of the season and the size of the catch; you can dredge the year round and you can take all you can get. Blackies have one drawback, a merchandising drawback—they aren't suited for the raw trade, the half-shell trade. You can only eat the young ones on the half shell—that is, the Little Necks, like these here. Young blackies are the finest-flavored clams in the world, in my opinion, but when they grow to cherrystone size they coarsen up. In addition they don't stand travel as good as bay clams; they're more perishable and their shells are brittle. All the clams in the bottom of this basket are probably broken and squashed. Blackies are perfect chowder clams—the old ones and the young ones—and that's what the Rhode

Islanders are selling them for. The clam-packing plants in Warren and Bristol and East Greenwich are buying all that's brought to their docks, and they're shucking and canning the entire catch. They're putting them up in gallon cans and selling them to hotels and restaurants and soup factories. They aren't going to fool with the half-shell trade. If the general public wants some for half-shell eating, unless they've got a friend in the business, I'm afraid they'll have to go to the docks and buy them off the boats, and that's a shame. Tommy, quit eating a moment and tell me what you think of these clams."

"The only thing that's got them beat in the shellfish line," said Mr. Maggiani, "is bay scallops eaten out of the shell—the whole raw scallop, and not just that scallop muscle that they fry in restaurants."

Mr. Flood was pleased. "I tell you, Tommy," he said, "it's been my experience that just about any animal that lives in a shell and comes out of salty water is good eating. Back in 1940 the oyster beds in Great Peconic Bay became infested with millions of gastropod pests called quarterdecks, a kind of limpet, the *Crepidula fornicata*. These pests fix themselves to oyster shells in great stacks and clusters, one on top of the other, and they smother the oysters to death. Around Christmas that winter I went out on the bay with a friend of mine, Drew Radel, whose family owns the Robbins Island beds. He fattens his stock in the North Race, a swift current of water between Great and Little Peconic, and they're the biggest, finest oysters in the United States. They're so big and fine that back before the war Drew used to ship hundreds of barrels by fast ocean liner to Paris, London, and Dublin, the chief oyster-eating cities of Europe. Drew took me to a ruined bed in the Race, a bed that had three thousand bushels of oysters in it, and thirteen thousand bushels of quarterdecks. It was enough to break your heart. I took a quarterdeck in my hand, an animal about an inch and a half long, and I thought to myself, 'I wonder how you taste.' I got my knife and I dug the meat out of one and I ate it, and Drew and the dredge-boat captain looked at me like I was an outcast from human society. I ate another, and I kept on eating, and I said to Drew, 'Drew, my boy,' I said, 'it's a sacrilegious thing to say, and I'm ashamed of myself, but the little buggers taste damned near as good as oysters.' He broke down and ate a few and he had to agree with me. Said they tasted to him like the tomalley of a lobster. I told him he should give them a French name and bribe the Waldorf-Astoria to put some on the menu at three dollars and a half a dozen. 'Create a demand for them,' I said, 'and you got the problem solved.' He said he wouldn't deal in the damned things for any amount of money. Anyhow, next year they vanished, the most of them. They come and go in cycles, like a good many pests."

THE WIND OFF THE RIVER shook Maggiani's windows. Mr. Flood went over to the stove, punched the fire, threw in a shovelful of coal, and returned to the clams. He was quiet for a while, brooding. Then he began to talk again. "I promised to tell you about Mr. Mooney's queer habit, didn't I?" he said to me.

"Yes, sir," I said.

"This is something I got no business telling a young man," Mr. Flood said, "but the pleasantest news to any human being over seventy-five is the news that some other human being around that age just died. That's provided the deceased ain't related, and sometimes even if he is. You put on a long face, and you tell everybody how sad and sorrowful it makes you feel, but you think to yourself, 'Well, I outlived him. Thank the Lord it was him and not me.' You think to yourself, 'One less. More room for me.' I've made quite a study of the matter, and I'm yet to find an agy man or any agy woman that don't feel the same deep down inside. It cheers you up somehow, God forgive me for saying so. I used to be ashamed of myself, but the way I figure, you can't help yourself, it's just nature. There's about a dozen and a half old crocks around seventy-five to eighty-five up at the Hartford, and here a few months back, the way it happens sometimes, they all got blue at once. Everybody had been sour-faced for days and getting sourer by the minute; they were all talked out; they had got on each other's nerves; a man would order a beer and go away down to the end of the bar by himself and drink it; you would say something to a man and he wouldn't answer you. It had just about got to the point where they were spitting in each other's eye. One afternoon around four I walked in and they were all up at the bar, the whole, entire mob, buying each other drinks, whacking each other on the shoulder. Two or three had reached the singing stage. Everybody was friends again. I asked one what happened, and he said to me, 'Didn't you hear the news? Old Dan up the street dropped dead an hour ago, the poor man. In the middle of cutting a customer's hair he keeled over and passed away.' Old Dan was a barber on Fulton Street; had a two-chair shop down here for fifty years; all the Hartford crowd went to him; a highly dignified man; everybody liked him; not an enemy in the world. I thought to myself, 'You heathen monsters! A poor old soul drops dead on the floor and it cheers you up!' But I got to be honest. In a minute I was hanging on the bar with the rest of them, going on about how sad it was, and what a fine man Old Dan had been, and how he'd given me a shave and a shampoo only the day before, and drinking more than I could handle, and feeling the best I had in I don't know when.

"Well, Mr. P. J. Mooney has an awful, awful case of what I'm talking about, the worst by far I ever saw. He comes downstairs in the morning in a hell of a hurry, and he grabs the *Times* and opens it up to the obituaries and death notices. The *Times* has the best death notices, all the details. And he sits there, drinking his coffee, happy, humming a song, reading up on who died since yesterday. And he talks to himself. He says, 'Well, my friend,' he says, looking at the picture of some poor deceased or other, 'I outlived you. You may have been one of the biggest investment bankers of our time, you may have left a thirty-million estate, you may have been a leader in social and financial circles in New York and Palm Beach, but I outlived you. You're in the funeral parlor, you old s.o.b., you and your thirty million, and here I am, P. J. Mooney, esquire, eating a fine big plate of ham and eggs, and I'm not going to have two cups of coffee this morning, I'm going to have three.' All that used to tickle me somewhat. I'd come downstairs and I'd say to him, 'Any good ones this morning, P. J.?' And he'd answer back, real cheerful, 'The president of a big steel company, well along in years, eighty-seven, fell and broke his hip, and a big doctor, a stomach specialist, seventy-three, had a stroke. It's sad,' he'd say, 'real sad.' And he'd sit there and give you all the details, the name of the undertaker that had the job, the name of the cemetery, how long was the final illness, who survived and the like of that.

"Here lately, the past month or so, in addition to studying the obituaries, P. J. has taken to studying the old men at the Hartford. I caught him several times staring at this one and that one, looking them over, eying them, and I knew for certain what he was doing; he was estimating how much longer they had to live. One day I caught him eying me. It gave me a turn. It made me uneasy. It upset me. And he's taken to inquiring about people's health; takes a great interest in how you feel. He says, 'Did you rest well last night?' And he says, 'You sure got the trembles. You can't drink nowhere near as much as you used to, can you?' And he says, 'Mr. Flood, it seems to me you're showing your age this morning. We're not getting any younger, none of us.' And last night he came out with a mighty upsetting question. 'Mr. Flood,' he said, 'if you were flat on your back with a serious illness and the doctor told you there was no hope left, what would you do?' And I said to him, 'Why, P. J., I would put on the God-damnedest exhibition that ever a dying man put on in the history of the human race. I would moan and groan and blubber and boohoo until the bricks came loose in the wall. I wouldn't remain in bed. I would get up from there and put me on a pair of striped pants and a box-back coat and I would grab the telephone and get in touch with preachers of all descriptions—preachers, priests, rabbis, the Salvation Army, the Mohammedans, Father Divine, any and all that would come, and I'd say to them, "Pray, brothers, pray! It can't do me no harm and it might possibly do me some good." And while they prayed I'd sit there and sing the "Rock of Ages" and drink all the liquor that the doctor would allow.' I thought that'd shut him up, but I was just wasting my breath. Next he wanted to know had I made my will, had I given much thought to what I wanted cut on my tomb-stone, did I have any favorite hymns I wanted sung at my funeral. 'Shut up,' I said to him, 'for the love of God, shut up!' And this morning I came down-stairs, and I had a hangover to begin with, a katzenjammer, and he had that estimating look in his eye, and he said to me, 'Good morning, Old Man Flood. How you feeling? You look a bit pale.' And I flew off the handle and danced around and made a holy show of myself. If he inquires about my health one more time, if he so much as says good morning, I'm going to answer him politely, like a gentleman, and I'm going to wait until he looks the other way, and then I'm going to pick up something heavy and lay him out."

"The way I look at it," said Mr. Maggiani, "those questions Mr. Mooney asks you, they're personal questions. I wouldn't stand for it."

"I'm not going to stand for it any longer," said Mr. Flood. "I'm going to put my foot down. All I want in this world is a little peace and quiet, and he gets me all raced up. Here a while back I heard a preacher talking on the radio about the peacefulness of the old, and I thought to myself, 'You ignorant man!' I'm ninety-four years old and I never yet had any peace, to speak of. My mind is just a turmoil of regrets. It's not what I did I regret, it's what I didn't do. Except for the bottle, I always walked the straight and narrow; a family man, a good provider, never cut up, never did ugly, and I regret it. In the summer of 1902 I came real close to getting in serious trouble with a married woman, but I had a fight with my conscience and my conscience won, and what's the result? I had two wives, good, Christian women, and I can't hardly remember what either of them looked like, but I can remember the face on that woman so clear it hurts, and there's never a day passes I don't think about her, and there's never a day passes I don't curse myself. 'What kind of a timid, dried-up, weevily fellow were you?' I say to myself. 'You should've said to hell with what's right and what's wrong, the devil take the hindmost. You'd have something to remember, you'd be happier now.' She's out in Woodlawn, six feet under, and she's been there twenty-two years, God rest her, and here I am, just an old, old man with nothing left but a belly and a brain and a dollar or two."

"Life is sad," said Mr. Maggiani.

"And the older I get," continued Mr. Flood, "the more impatient I get. I got no time to waste on fools. There's a young Southern fellow drops into the Hartford barroom every night before he gets on the 'L'; comes from Alabama; works in one of those cotton offices on Hanover Square. Seemed to be a likable young fellow. I got in the habit of having a whiskey with him. He'd buy a round, I'd buy a round. Night before last, when he dropped in, I was sitting at a table with a colored man. When I was in the house-wrecking business, this colored man was my boss foreman. He was in my employ for thirty-six years; practically ran the business; one of the finest men I've ever known; raised eight children; one's a doctor. In the old days, when my second wife was still alive, he and his wife came to our house for dinner, and me and my wife went to his house for dinner; played cards, told stories, listened to the phonograph. When I sold the business, I gave him a pension, an annuity. He bought a little farm on Long Island, and whenever he's in town he pays me a visit and we talk about the days gone by. Tommy, you remember Peter Stetson. He's been in here with me."

"Sure," said Mr. Maggiani. "Fellow that runs the duck farm."

"That's right," said Mr. Flood. "Well, Pete and I finished our talk, and I walked to the door with him, and we shook hands, and he left. And I went over to the bar to have a drink with this young Southern fellow, and he says, 'That was a nigger you were sitting down with, wasn't it?' And I said, 'That was an old, old friend of mine.' And he began to talk some ugly talk about the colored people, and I shut him right up. 'I'm an old-time New Yorker,' I said to him, 'the melting-pot type, the Tammany type before Tammany went to seed, all for one, one for all, a man's race and color is his own business, and I be damned if I'll listen to that kind of talk.' And he says, 'You're a trouble-maker. What race do you belong to, anyhow?' 'The human race,' I said. 'I come from the womb and I'm bound for the tomb, the same as you, the same as King George the Six, the same as Johnny Squat. And furthermore,' I said, 'I'll never take another drink with you. It would be beneath me to do so.' Now that's a heathen kind of thing to happen in New York City. I'm going over and talk to the Mayor one of these days, tell him about a plan I have. I got a plan for a parade. The population is all split up; they don't even parade with each other. The Italians parade on Columbus Day, the Poles parade on Pulaski Day, the Irish parade on St. Patrick's Day, and all like that. My plan is to have a citywide Human Race Parade, an all-day, all-night parade up Fifth Avenue. The only qualification you'll need to march in this parade, you have to belong to the human race. The cops even, they won't stand and watch, they'll get right in and march. Tommy, how about you, would you march in the Human Race Parade?"

"It would depend on the weather," said Mr. Maggiani.

Mr. Flood sighed and tossed his gut-blade on the counter. "I'm full," he said. "I've had my bait of clams."

"Me, too," said Mr. Maggiani. "There's no law says we got to make pigs of ourselves."

Mr. Flood got a rag and a pan of water and cleaned off the oilcloth counter, and I gathered up the empty shells and put them in a trash bucket. Mr. Maggiani carried what was left of the basket of blackies back to the coldroom. Then the three of us sat down by the stove. Mr. Maggiani put a pot of coffee on the hob. We heard steps in the hall, the door opened, and in came a friend of Mr. Flood's, a grim old Yankee named Jack Murchison, who is a waiter in Libby's Oyster House. Libby's is one of the few New England restaurants in the city. It was established on Fulton Street in 1840 by Captain Oliver Libby of Wellfleet, Cape Cod. It is unpretentious, its chefs and waiters are despotic and opinionated but highly skilled, it broils or boils or poaches ninety-nine fish orders for every one it fries, it has Daniel Webster fish chowder on Wednesdays and Fridays, and it has New England clam chowder every day. On its menu is a statement of policy: "OPEN TO 8 P.M. NOT RESPONSIBLE FOR PERSONAL PROPERTY. NO MAN-HATTAN CLAM CHOWDER SERVED IN HERE."

"Been down to the river for a breath of air," Mr. Murchison said. "Sat on the stringpiece for fifteen minutes and I'm cold to the bone."

"Draw up a chair, Jack," said Mr. Flood, "and take the weight off your feet."

Mr. Murchison lifted the tails of his overcoat and stood with his back to the stove for a few min-utes. Then he sat down and sighed with satisfaction. "Hugh," he said to Mr. Flood, "got something I want to show you." He took his wallet from a hip pocket, drew out a newspaper clipping, and gave it to me to pass over to Mr. Flood, who was sitting on the other side of the stove. It was a clipping of Lucius Beebe's column, "This New York," in the *Herald Tribune*.

Mr. Flood glanced at it and said, "Oh, God,

what's this? Is he one of those ignorant fellows writes about restaurants in the papers, ohs and ahs about everything they put before him? Every paper nowadays has a fellow writing about restaurants, an expert giving his opinion, a fellow that if he was out of a job and went to a restaurant to get one, this expert on cooking, this Mr. Know-it-all, the practical knowledge he has, why, they wouldn't trust him to peel the potatoes for a stew."

"This gentleman is a goormy," said Mr. Murchison. "Go ahead and read what he says."

Mr. Flood read a paragraph or two. Then he groaned and handed the clipping to me. "God defend us, son," he said. "Read this."

In the column, Mr. Beebe described a dinner that had been "run up" for him and a friend by Edmond Berger, the *chef de cuisine* of the Colony Restaurant. He gave the menu in full. One item, the fish course, was "Fillet de Sole en Bateau Beebe." "The sole, courteously created in the name of this department by Chef Berger for the occasion," Mr. Beebe wrote, "was a delicate fillet superimposed on a half baked banana and a trick worth remembering."

"Good God A'mighty!" said Mr. Flood.

"Sounds nice, don't it?" asked Mr. Murchison. "A half baked bananny with a delicate piece of flounder superimposed on the top of it. While he was at it, why didn't he tie a red ribbon around it?"

"Next they'll be putting a cherry on boiled codfish," said Mr. Flood. "How would that be, a delicate piece of codfish with a cherry superimposed on the top of it?"

The two old men cackled.

"Tell me the truth, Hugh," said Mr. Murchison, "what in the world do you think of a thing like that?"

"I tell you what I think," said Mr. Flood. "I got my money in the Corn Exchange Bank. And if I was to go into some restaurant and see the president of the Corn Exchange Bank eating a thing like that, why, I would turn right around and walk out of there, and I'd hightail it over to the Corn Exchange Bank and draw out every red cent. It would destroy my confidence."

"President, hell," said Mr. Murchison. "If I was to see the janitor of the Corn Exchange Bank eating a thing like that, I'd draw *my* money out."

"Of course," said Mr. Flood, "you got to take into consideration this fellow is a gourmet. A thing like that is just messy enough to suit a gourmet. They got bellies like schoolgirls; they can eat anything, just so it's messy."

"We get a lot of goormies in Libby's," said Mr. Murchison. "I can spot a goormy right off. Moment he sits down he wants to know do we have any boolybooze."

"Bouillabaisse," said Mr. Flood.

"Yes," said Mr. Murchison, "and I tell him, 'Quit showing off! We don't carry no boolybooze. Never did. There's a time and a place for everything. If you was to go into a restaurant in France,' I ask him, 'would you call for some Daniel Webster fish chowder?' I love a hearty eater, but I do despise a goormy. All they know is boolybooze and pompano and something that's out of season, nothing else will do. And when they get through eating they don't settle their check and go on about their business. No, they sit there and deliver you a lecture on what they et, how good it was, how it was almost as good as a piece of fish they had in the Caffy dee lah Pooty-doo in Paris, France, on January 16, 1928;

they remember every meal they ever et, or make out they do. And every goormy I ever saw is an expert on herbs. Herbs, herbs, herbs! If you let one get started on the subject of herbs he'll talk you deef, dumb, and blind. Way I feel about herbs, on any fish I ever saw, pepper and salt and a spoon of melted butter is herbs aplenty."

"Let's see that clipping again," Mr. Flood said. He took the Beebe column and read it slowly from start to finish. Then he handed it back to me. "Burn a rag," he said.

Mr. Maggiani lifted the pot of coffee off the hob and poured us each a mug. Then he stepped over to the counter and got his Scotch bottle. There was an ounce or two left in it, and he poured this into Mr. Murchison's coffee.

"Much obliged, Tommy," said Mr. Murchison. "It was cold out."

"I know it," said Mr. Maggiani. "I heard the wind whistling." Mr. Maggiani turned to Mr. Flood. "Hugh," he said, "there's something I was going to ask you. You've got enough money put away you could live high if you wanted to. Why in God's name do you live in a little box of a room in a back-street hotel and hang out in the fish market when you could go down to Miami, Florida, and sit in the sun?"

Mr. Flood bit the end off one of his sixty-five-cent cigars and spat it into the scuttle. He held a splinter in the stove until it caught fire, and then he lit the cigar. "Tommy, my boy," he said, "I don't know. Nobody knows why they do anything. I could give you one dozen reasons why I prefer the Fulton Fish Market to Miami, Florida, and most likely none would be the right one. The right reason is something obscure and way off and I probably don't even know it myself. It's like the old farmer who wouldn't tell the drummer the time of day."

"What are you talking about?" asked Mr. Maggiani.

"It's an old, old story," Mr. Flood said. "I've heard it told sixteen different ways. I even heard a muxed-up version one night years ago in a vaude-ville show. I'll tell it the way my daddy used to tell it. There was an old farmer lived beside a little branch-line railroad in south Jersey, and every so often he'd get on the train and go over to Trenton and buy himself a crock of applejack. He'd buy it right at the distillery door, the old Bossert & Stockton Apple Brandy Distillery, and save himself a penny or two. One morning he went to Trenton and bought his crock, and that afternoon he got on the train for the trip home. Just as the train pulled out, he took his watch from his vest pocket, a fine gold watch in a fancy hunting case, and he looked at it, and then he snapped it shut and put it back in his pocket. And there was a drummer sitting across the aisle. This drummer leaned over and said, 'Friend, what time is it?' The farmer took a look at him and said, 'Won't tell you.' The drummer thought he was hard of hearing and spoke louder. 'Friend,' he shouted out, 'what time is it?' 'Won't tell you,' said the farmer. The drummer thought a moment and then he said, 'Friend, all I asked was the time of day. It don't cost anything to tell the time of day.' 'Won't tell you,' said the farmer. 'Well, look here, for the Lord's sake,' said the drummer, 'why won't you tell me the time of day?' 'If I was to tell you the time of day,' the farmer said, 'we'd get into a conversation, and I got a crock of spirits down on the floor between my feet, and in a minute I'm going to take a drink, and if we were having a conversation I'd ask you to take a drink with me, and you would, and presently I'd take another, and I'd ask you to do the same, and you would, and we'd get to drinking, and by and by the train'd pull up to the stop where I get off, and I'd ask you why don't you get off and spend the afternoon with me, and you would, and we'd walk up to my house and sit on the front porch and drink and sing, and along about dark my old lady would come out and ask you to take supper with us, and you would, and after supper I'd ask if you'd care to drink some more, and you would, and it'd get to be real late and I'd ask you to spend the night in the spare room, and you would, and along about two o'clock in the morning I'd get up to go to the pump, and I'd pass my daughter's room, and there you'd be, in there with my daughter, and I'd have to turn the bureau upside down and get out my pistol, and my old lady would have to get dressed and hitch up the horse and go down the road and get the preacher, and I don't want no God-damned son-in-law who don't own a watch.'"—*(1944)*

MR. FLOOD'S PARTY

MR. FLOOD WAS NINETY-FIVE YEARS OLD on the twenty-seventh of July, 1945. Three evenings beforehand, on the twenty-fourth, he gave a birthday party in his room at the Hartford House. "I don't believe in birthday parties never did but some do and I will have one this time to suit myself if it kills me," he wrote on a penny postal, inviting me. "Will be obliged to have it on the 24th as I promised my daughter Louise in South Norwalk I would be with her and my grandchildren and great grandchildren on my birthday itself. Couldn't get out of it. And due to I can't seem to find any pure Scotch whiskey any more it has got so it takes me two or three days to get over a toot. Louise is deadset against whiskey talk talk talk and I know better than to show up in

South Norwalk with a katzenjammer. I will expect you. It will not be a big party just a few windbags from the fish market. Also Tom Bethea. He is an old, old friend of my family. He is an undertaker. The party will start around six and it is immaterial to me when it stops. I am well and trust you are the same."

I walked up Peck Slip around six-thirty on the evening of the twenty-fourth, and the peace and mystery of midnight was already over everything; work begins long before daybreak in the fish market and ends in the middle of the afternoon. There wasn't a human being in sight, or an automobile. The old pink-brick fish houses on both sides of the Slip had been shuttered and locked, the sidewalks had been flushed, and there were easily two hundred gulls from the harbor walking around in the gutters, hunting for fish scraps. The gulls came right up to the Hartford's stoop. They were big gulls and they were hungry and anxious and as dirty as buzzards. Also, in the quiet street, they were spooky. I stood on the stoop and watched them for a few minutes, and then I went into the hotel's combined lobby and barroom. Gus Trein, the manager, was back of the bar. There were no customers and he was working on his books; he had two ledgers and a spindle of bills before him. I asked if Mr. Flood was upstairs. "He is," said Mr. Trein, "what's left of him. Are you going to his party?" I said I was. "In that case," he said, "hold your hat. He was in and out all afternoon, toting things up to his room, and he had three bottles of whiskey one trip. The last time he came in, half an hour ago, Birdy Treppel was with him—the old fishwife from the Slip. He had a smoked eel about a yard long in one hand and a box of cigars in the other, and he was singing 'Down, Down Among the Dead Men,' and Birdy had him by the elbow, helping him up the stairs."

One of Mr. Flood's closest friends, Matthew T. Cusack, was sitting on the bottom of the stairs in the rear of the lobby. He had one shoe off and was prizing a tack out of it with his pocketknife. Mr. Cusack is a portly, white-haired old Irish-American, a retired New York City policeman. He is a watchman for the Fulton Market Fishmongers Association; he sits all night in a sprung swivel chair beside a window in a shack on the fish pier. In the last six or seven months, Mr. Cusack's personality has undergone an extraordinary change. He was once a hearty man. He laughed a lot and he was a big eater and straight-whiskey drinker. He had a habit of remarking to bartenders that he didn't see any sense in mixing whiskey with water, since the whiskey was already wet. At a clambake for marketmen and their families in East Islip, in the summer of 1944, he ate three hundred and sixty-six Great South Bay quahogs, one for every day in the year (it was a leap year), and put four rock-broiled lobsters on top of them. He has a deep chest and a good baritone, and at market gatherings he always stood up and sang "The Broken Home," "Frivolous Sal," and "Just Fill Me One Glass More." In recent months, however, he has been gloomy and irritable and pious; he is worried about his health and believes that he may have a heart attack at any moment and drop dead. He was in vigorous health until last Christmas, when the Fishery Council, the market's chamber of commerce, gave him a present, a radio for his shack. Aside from listening in barrooms to broadcasts of championship prizefights, Mr. Cusack had never before paid any attention to the radio, but he soon got to be a fan.

He got so he would keep his radio on all night. A program he especially likes is sponsored by a company that sells a medicine for the acid indigestion. Around the middle of February, he developed the acid indigestion and began to take this medicine. Then, one morning in March, on his way home from the market, he was troubled by what he describes as "a general run-down feeling." At first he took it for granted that this was caused by the acid indigestion, but that night, while listening to a radio health chat, he came to the conclusion that he had a heart condition. He is fascinated by health chats; they make him uneasy, but he dials them in from stations all over the country. He got over the run-down feeling but continued to brood about his heart. He went to a specialist, who made a series of cardiograms and told him that he was in good shape for a man of his age and weight. He is still apprehensive. He says he suspects he has a rare condition that can't be detected by the cardiograph. He never smiles, he has a frightened stare, and his face is set and gray. He walks slowly, inching along with an almost effortless shuffle, to avoid straining his heart muscles. When he is not at work, he spends most of the time lying flat on his back in bed with his feet propped up higher than his head. He takes vitamin tablets, a kind that is activated *and* mineralized. Also, twice a day, he takes a medicine that is guaranteed to alkalize the system. The officials of the Council are sorry they gave him the radio. Edmond Irwin, the executive secretary, ran into him on the pier a while back and told him so. "Why, what in the world are you talking about?" Mr. Cusack asked. "That radio probably saved my life. If it wasn't for that radio, I might've dropped dead already. I didn't start taking care of myself until those health chats woke me up to the danger I was in."

I went on back to the rear of the lobby and spoke to Mr. Cusack, but he didn't look up or answer. He had the stairs blocked or I would have gone on past him. After he got the tack out of his shoe, he stood up and grunted. His face was heavy with worry. We shook hands, and I asked him if he was going to Mr. Flood's party or coming from it. "Going, God help me," he said, "and I dread it. I feel like I ought to pay my respects to Hugh, but I dread the stairs. A poor old man in my condition, it's taking my life in my hands." The Hartford is five floors high and it doesn't have an elevator. Mr. Flood's room is on the top floor. I stood aside and waited for Mr. Cusack to start up, but he said, "You go ahead. I'm going to take my time. It'll take me half an hour and when I get to the top I'll most likely drop dead."

MR. FLOOD HAS A CORNER ROOM, overlooking the Slip. The door was open. His room is usually in a mess and he had obviously had it straightened up for the party. There was a freshly ironed counterpane on his brass bed. His library had been neatly arranged on top of his tin, slatbound trunk; it consists of a Bible, a set of Mark Twain, and two thick United States Bureau of Fisheries reference books, "Fishes of the Gulf of Maine" and "Fishes of Chesapeake Bay." His collection of sea shells and river shells had been laid out on the hearth of the boarded-up fireplace. Ordinarily, his books and shells are scattered all over the floor. On the marble mantelpiece were three small cast-iron statues—a bare-knuckle pug with his fists cocked, a running horse with its mane streaming, and an American eagle. These came off one of the magnificent fire escapes on the Dover

Street side of the old *Police Gazette* building, which is at Dover and Pearl, in the fish-market neighborhood. (Mr. Flood is sentimental about the stone and iron ornaments on many buildings down in the old city, and he thinks they should be preserved. He once wrote the Museum of the City of New York suggesting that the owners of the *Gazette* building be asked to donate the fire-escape ornaments to the Museum. "Suppose this bldg. is torn down," he wrote. "All that beautiful iron work will disappear into scrap. If the owners do not see fit to donate, I am a retired house-wrecker and I could go there in the dead of night with a monkey-wrench and blow-torch and use my own discretion.") Above the mantelpiece hung a lithograph of Franklin D. Roosevelt, a Thomas Rowlandson aquatint of some scuffling fishwives in Billingsgate that came off a calendar, and a framed beatitude: "BLESSED IS THE MAN WHO DOES NOT BELLYACHE—ELBERT HUBBARD." In the middle of the room stood an ugly old marble-top table, the kind that has legs shaped like the claws of a dragon, each claw grasping a glass ball. There was a clutter on the table—a bottle of Scotch, a pitcher of water, a bucket of ice, a box of cigars, a

crock of pickled mussels, a jar of marinated her-
rings, a smoked eel, a wire basket of sea urchins, two
loaves of Italian bread, some lemons, and a stack of
plates. The sea urchins were wet and dripping.

There were four people sitting around the
table—Mr. Flood, Mrs. Treppel, a salesman of
fishing-boat hardware named Ben Fass, and an old
man I had never seen before. Mrs. Treppel had
Commodore, the Hartford's big black cat, on her
lap; she had given it the head of the eel. Mrs.
Treppel was still in her market clothes. She wore a
full-length coat-apron over her dress and she had
on knee boots and a man's stiff straw hat; this is the
uniform of the boss fishmonger. The hat was on the
side of her head. Mrs. Treppel is stout, red-cheeked,
and good-natured. Even so, as a day wears on, she
becomes quite quarrelsome; she says she quarrels
just to keep her liver regulated. "Quarreling is the
only exercise I take," she says. She is a widow in her
late sixties, she has worked in the market since she
was a young woman, and she is greatly respected,
especially by the old-timers; to them, she is the very
embodiment of the primary, basic, fundamental
Fulton Fish Market virtue—the ability to look after

Number One. "Birdy Treppel likes to run her mouth, and she sometime sounds a little foolish," I once heard one old boss fishmonger say to another, "but don't ever underestimate her. She could buy or sell half the people down here, including me." Mrs. Treppel owns a couple of the old buildings on Peck Slip, she has money in a cooperage that builds boxes and barrels for the fish trade; she owns a share in a dragger, the *Betty Parker*, which runs out of Stonington, Connecticut; and she keeps a fresh-water stall on the Slip, dealing mainly in carp, whitefish, and pike, the species that are used in gefüllte fish. Mr. Fass is known in the market as Ben the Knifeman. He is slight, edgy, and sad-eyed, a disappointed man, and he blames all his troubles on cellophane. He says that he was ruined by cellophane, and he sometimes startles people by muttering, "Whoever he is, wherever he is, God damn the man that invented cellophane!" He once was a salesman for a sausage-casings broker in Gansevoort Market, selling sheep intestines to manufacturers of frankfurters. He enjoyed this work. Ten years ago many manufacturers began using cellophane instead of intestines for casings, calling their product "skinless" frankfurters, and in 1937 Mr. Fass was laid off. He became an outside man for a Water Street fishing-boat supply house, which is owned by an uncle of his. Carrying samples in a suitcase, he goes aboard trawlers and draggers at the pier and sits down with the captains and takes orders for knives, honing steels, scalers, bait grinders, swordfish darts, fog bells, and similar hardware.

Mr. Fass and Mr. Flood are good friends, which is puzzling. Mr. Fass has no interest in boats, he dislikes the fish market, and he despises fish. He is outspoken about it; not long ago he lost one of his best customers by remarking that he would rather have one thin cut off a tough rib roast than all the fish God ever made. Mr. Flood, on the other hand, believes that people would be much better off in mind and body if they ate meat on Fridays and fish all the rest of the week. I have known Mr. Flood for nine years, but I found out only recently how he arrived at this conclusion. From 1885 until 1930, when he retired, the offices of his firm, the H. G. Flood Demolition & Salvage Co., Inc., were on Franklin Square, a couple of blocks from the fish market. In the winter of 1885, soon after moving there, he observed that there was a predominance of elderly and aged men among the fishmongers. "I began to step up to these men and inquire about their ages," he told me. "There were scores in their eighties and dozens in their nineties and spry old crocks that had hit a hundred weren't rare at all. One morning I saw a fist fight between two men in their nineties. They slapped each other from one end of the pier to the other, and it was a better fight than many a fight I paid to see. Another morning I saw the fellows shaking hands with a man of eighty-seven and it turned out his wife had just had a baby boy. All these men were tough and happy and full of the old Adam, and all were big fish eaters, and I thought to myself, 'Flood, no doubt about it, you have hit on a secret.'" Since that winter he has seldom eaten anything but seafood.

When I came into the room, Mr. Flood had just begun a song. He has a bullfrog bass, and he sang loudly and away off key. He had a highball in his left hand and a cigar in his right, and he kept time with the cigar as he sang:

"Come, let us drink while we have breath,

For there's no drinking after death
And he that will this health deny,
Down among the dead men,
Down among the dead men—"

I was quite sure that he would put in more "downs" than the song called for, and I counted them. There were eleven, and each was louder than the one before it:

"Down, down, down, down, down,
down, down, down, down, down,
Down among the dead men
Let him lie!"

Mr. Flood's guests banged on the marble-top with their glasses, and he beamed. He was looking well. His friendly, villainous eyes were bright and his face was so tanned that the liver freckles on his cheeks didn't show; he carries a blanket down to the pier and lies in the sun an hour or two on good afternoons. He had on a white linen suit and there was a red rosebud in his lapel. I tried to congratulate him on his birthday. He wouldn't let me. "Thanks, my boy," he said, "but it's too early for that. I just got started. Wait'll I hit a hundred." He turned to the stranger at the table. "This is Tom Bethea," he said. "Tom's an undertaker up in Chelsea, my old neighborhood. Tom's wife and my second wife were great friends. We belong to the same Baptist church, only he goes and I don't." Mr. Bethea was roly-poly, moon-faced, and bald. His eyes were remarkably distrustful. He wore a blue serge suit that was so tight it made me uncomfortable to look at him. He had a glass about a third full of straight whiskey in one hand. With the other, he was plucking mussels out of the crock and popping them into his mouth as if they were peanuts. He seemed offended by Mr. Flood's introduction. "I'm *not* an undertaker," he said. "I'm an embalmer. I've told you that time and time again, and I do wish you'd get it straight."

"Whichever it is," said Mr. Flood. He turned to me and said, "Pull up a chair and fix yourself a drink. I got something I want to show you." He took a photograph out of his wallet and handed it to me. It was a photograph of a horse, an old white sway-backed horse. "Look at it and pass it around," he said. "I was going through some papers in my trunk the other day and came across it. Thought I'd lost it years ago. It's a snapshot of a horse named Sam. Sam was a highly unusual horse and I want to tell about him. He was owned by George Still, fellow that ran Still's Oyster and Chop House. Still's was on Third Avenue, between Seventeenth and Eighteenth, middle of the block, east side of the avenue. It opened in the eighteen-fifties—1853, I think it was—and it closed in 1922 because of prohibition, and it was the finest oyster house the country ever had. It was a hangout for rich old goaty high-living men—Tammany bosses and the like of that. Some of them could taste an oyster and examine the shell and tell you what bed it came out of; I'm pretty good at that myself. And it got crowds of out-of-towners, especially people from Boston, Philadelphia, Baltimore, Norfolk, and New Orleans, the big oyster-eating cities. Mr. Still handled a wider variety of oysters than any restaurant or hotel in the world, before or since. He had them out of dozens of beds. From New Jersey he had Shrewsburys and Maurice River Coves. From Rhode Island he had Narragansetts and Wickfords. From Massachusetts he had Cotuits and Buzzards Bays and Cape Cods. From Virginia—they were very fine—he had Chincoteagues and Lynnhavens and Pokomokes and Mobjacks and Horn Harbors and York Rivers and Hampton Bars and Rappahannocks. From Maryland he had Goose Creeks. From Delaware he had Bombay Hooks. From New York—the finest of all—he had Blue Points and Mattitucks and Saddle Rocks and Robbins Islands and Diamond Points and Fire Places and Montauks and Hog Necks and Millponds and Fire Island Salts and Rockaways and Shinnecocks. I love those good old oyster names. When I feel my age weighing me down, I recite them to myself and I feel better. Some of them don't exist any more. The beds were ruined. Cities grew up nearby and the water went bad. But there was a time when you could buy them all in Still's."

"Oh, God, Hughie," said Mrs. Treppel, "it *was* a wonderful place. I remember it well. It had a white marble bar for the half-shell trade, and there were barrels and barrels and barrels of oysters stood up behind this bar, and everything was nice and plain and solid—no piddling around, no music to frazzle your nerves, no French on the bill of fare; you got what you went for."

"I remember Still's, too," said Mr. Bethea. "Biggest lobster I ever saw, I saw it in there. Weighed thirty-four pounds. Took two men to hold it. It was a hen lobster. It wasn't much good— too coarse and stringy—but it was full of coral and tomalley and it scared the women and it was educational."

"That's right," said Mr. Flood. "That's the way it was." He poured himself a drink. "In addition to the restaurant," he continued, "Mr. Still did a wholesale oyster business in a triple-decked barge that was docked year in and year out at a pier at the foot of Pike Street, upriver from the fish market. The barge was his warehouse. In the old days all the wholesalers operated that way; they brought their stock in from the beds in schooners that'd come alongside the barges and unload. At the time I'm speaking of—in 1912—there were fourteen barges at Pike Street, all in a row and all painted as loud and bedizy and fancy-colored as possible, the same as gypsy wagons; that was the custom. George Still is dead, God rest him, but the business is there yet. His family runs it. It's one of the biggest shellfish concerns in the city, and it's right there in the old barge, head office and all—George M. Still, Incorporated, Planters of Diamond Point Oysters. Still's barge is the only one left, and it's a pretty one. It's painted green and yellow and it's got scroll-saw work all over the front of it.

"Back in 1912, Mr. Still delivered his oysters to hotels and restaurants and groceries with horse-drawn drays. He owned nine horses and he thought a lot of them. Every summer he gave them two weeks off on a farm he had in New Jersey. One of those horses was Sam. Sam was the oldest. In fact, he was twenty-two years old, and that's a ripe old advanced age for a horse. Sam was just about worn out. His head hung low, his eyes were sleepy and sad, and there wasn't hardly any life in him at all. If some horseflies lit on him, he didn't even have the energy to switch his tail and knock them off. He just poked along, making short hauls and waiting for the day to end. Mr. Still had made up his mind to retire Sam to New Jersey for good, but he was one of those that puts things off; tomorrow will do.

"Sam's driver was a man named Woodrow and he was attached to Sam. Sam was noted for his good disposition, but one morning in October,

1912, Woodrow went to put the harness on Sam and Sam kicked at him. It was the first time that ever happened. Next morning Sam was worse. Every single time Woodrow got near, Sam kicked. He was so old and awkward he always missed, but he kept on trying; he did his best. Every day that passed, Sam got more free and easy. He'd rear back in the shafts and tangle up the strappings on his harness, and sometimes Woodrow would tell him to whoa and he'd keep right on going until he was good and damn ready to whoa. He got a mean look in his eye and he kept his head up and he walked faster and faster. He'd toss his head to and fro and dance along like a yearling. One day, all of a sudden, up on Sixth Avenue, he started running after a bay mare that was hauling a laundry wagon. It was all Woodrow could do to pull him up. And Sam kept on doing this. Every day or so he'd catch sight of a mare somewhere up ahead and he'd whinny and whicker and break into a fast trot and Woodrow would have to brace himself against the footboard and seesaw on the lines and curse and carry on to stop him. Sometimes a crowd would collect and cheer Sam on. Woodrow worried about

Sam, and so did Mr. Still, but they didn't know what to do. They couldn't figure him out.

"One of the places that Woodrow and Sam made a daily delivery was a chop house on Maiden Lane. Sam would stand at the curb and Woodrow would shoulder a barrel of oysters off the dray and roll it in. The cashier of this chop house was an old lady and every morning she'd step out to the curb and pat Sam's nose and coo at him and give him sugar. She'd been doing it for years. She was one of those old ladies that just can't leave horses alone. One morning she came out, cooing, and she put her hand out to pat Sam and Sam bit her. He bit her on the hand and he bit her on the wrist and he bit her on the arm. She was all skint up. As you might expect, a great deal of screeching took place. They sent for a doctor, but that didn't quiet the old lady. According to Woodrow, she kept screeching she didn't want a doctor, she wanted a lawyer.

"Woodrow led Sam back to the barge and broke the news to Mr. Still that he had a damage suit on his hands. Mr. Still called in a veterinarian to see could he find out what was the matter with Sam, what ailed the old fool. The veterinarian looked

Sam over and he punched and he thumped and he put his head against Sam's belly and listened. He said he couldn't find anything wrong except extreme old age. Then he happened to look into Sam's feed bag, and what in hell and be damned was in there, mixed in with the oats, only some shucked oysters. They weren't little nubby oysters; they were great big Mattitucks. And what's more, Sam was eating them. He was eating them and enjoying them. The veterinarian stood there and he looked at Sam and he said, 'Well, I be good God damned!' He said he'd run into some odd and unusual horses in his practice but that Sam was certainly the first horse he'd run into that'd eat oysters.

"Mr. Still called his help together and inquired did anybody know who put the oysters in Sam's feed bag. Finally one of the oyster shuckers confessed he did it. Said he just wanted to see what would happen. Said he'd been slipping them in for about a month. Said he'd go out on the pier, where Sam was hitched between hauls, and he'd make believe he was petting Sam, and he'd slip the oysters into Sam's feed bag. Said he started with one oyster a day and worked up to where he was giving him four and five dozen a day. Mr. Still was put out; at the same time, somehow, he was proud of Sam. He decided to fire the shucker and send Sam to hell and gone to New Jersey, but he changed his mind. What he did, he cut Sam down to one dozen oysters a day. That worked out all right. It wasn't too few, it wasn't too many. It was just enough to keep Sam brisk and frisky, but it wasn't enough to make him cut up and do ugly. People would come from all over the market just to see Sam get his one dozen oysters. Everything was just fine until Christmas Eve. You know how it is on Christmas Eve; people get high-spirited. And you can just imagine how high-spirited they get around an oyster barge on Christmas Eve. When it came time to feed Sam, the fellows got generous and gave him six or seven dozen oysters, compliments of the season. And that night Woodrow was driving Sam back to the stable and Sam caught sight of a mare about three blocks up and he took out after her and there was ice on the street and he slipped and broke a leg and God knows they hated to do it, but they had to shoot him."

A glint came into Mr. Bethea's eyes. "Hugh," he said, "I was just thinking. Suppose you took and fed a race horse on oysters! I bet you could make a lot of money that way."

Mr. Flood snickered. "Tom," he said, "there's a certain race horse on the New York tracks right now that's an oyster eater. He's owned by an oysterman here in the market, but the way I understand it, just to throw people off that might possibly get thoughts in their head, he's registered in the name of a distant cousin of this oysterman's wife. He's not much of a horse—no looks, no style; he only cost eleven hundred dollars—but he wins every race they want him to win. They don't let him win every race he runs; that'd look peculiar."

I watched Mr. Flood's face. It was impassive.

"They pick a day," he continued, "and two days in advance they start feeding him raw oysters or raw clams, according to season. They experimented and found he runs about as fast on clams as he does on oysters. They give him five dozen the first day, eight dozen the second day, and one dozen the morning of the race. He always comes through; you just get a bet down and think no more about it. I don't know how many are in on it. I do know that this oysterman and all his friends were rolling in money. He was nice enough to let me and Birdy in on it. Whenever the horse is ready to run an oyster-fed race, we get notified, and naturally we've picked up a dollar or two ourselves."

"Hugh Griffin Flood!" said Mrs. Treppel. "I'm shocked and surprised at you. You were told about that horse in the strictest confidence. It's a highly confidential matter, and you know you shouldn't talk about it. Suppose it gets out. They'll be stuffing all the race horses full of oysters, and then where'll we be?"

"I know, Birdy, I know," said Mr. Flood. "I'm sorry. Anyhow, I didn't tell the name of the horse."

"You keep your big mouth shut from now on," said Mrs. Treppel.

"Speaking of the old days," said Mr. Bethea, "it seems to me businessmen were different in the old days. They had the milk of human kindness in them. Like George Still. Like the way he gave his dray horses a vacation."

"It's the truth, Tom," said Mr. Flood. "They weren't always and eternally thinking of the almighty dollar."

"I was doing business in the old days," said Mrs.

Treppel, "and that's something I never noticed."

"You always remember the bad, Birdy," said Mr. Flood. "You never remember the good."

"I don't know about that," said Mrs. Treppel. "Take for example, were you acquainted with A. C. Lowry that they called the finnan-haddie king?"

"I was," said Mr. Flood. "Old Gus Lowry." He nodded his head. "Gus was a fine man," he said, "a fine man."

"He was like hell," said Mrs. Treppel. "He was the meanest man ever did business in this market. He was the lowest of the low."

"He was," said Mr. Flood, reversing his judgment without batting an eye. "He was indeed."

"What form did his meanness take?" asked Mr. Bethea.

"Well, to begin with," Mrs. Treppel said, "you couldn't trust him. You couldn't trust his weights or his invoices or the condition of his fish, not that that was so highly unusual down here and not that people necessarily looked down on him for that. After all, this isn't the New York Stock Exchange, where everybody is upright and honest and trustworthy, or so I have been told—this is the Fulton

Fish Market. No, it wasn't his crookedness, it was the way he conducted himself in general that turned people against him. He was stingy. He believed everybody was stealing from him. He treated his help in such a way they didn't know if they were going or coming. And he grumbled about this and he complained about that from morning to night; everything he et disagreed with him. I worked for him once—he had a fresh-water branch on the Slip around 1916 and I had charge of it. I worked for him a year and a half and it aged me before my time; when I took that job I was just a girl and when I gave it up I was an old, old woman. Gus was into everything. He did a general salt-water business. He owned a trawler. He handled Staten Island oysters and guaranteed they came from Norfolk, Virginia. And he had the biggest smoking loft in the market—eels, haddies, kippers, and bloaters. He was an old bachelor. He had a nephew keeping books for him, Charlie Titus, his sister's son, and everybody was sorry for Charlie. It was understood that Charlie was to inherit the business, and God knows it was a good sound business, but the beating he took, we wondered if it was worth it. Charlie was real polite, Uncle this and Uncle that, but it didn't do no good. Three or four times a year, at least, Gus would get it in his head that Charlie was falsifying the books. He'd see something in Charlie's figures that didn't look just right and it'd make him happy. 'I've caught you now!' he'd say. 'I've caught you now!' Then he'd grab the telephone and call in a firm of certified public accountants. Those damned C.P.A.s were in and out of the office all the time. They'd go over Charlie's books and they'd try their best, but they couldn't ever find anything wrong, and it'd make Gus so mad he'd put his head down on the desk and cry. 'You low-down thief,' he'd say to Charlie, 'you're stealing from me, and I know you are. You got some secret way of doing it. My own flesh and blood, and you're stealing every cent I got.' Charlie would say, 'Now, Uncle Gus, that's just not so,' and Gus would say, 'Shut up!' And Charlie would shut up. I remember one morning Gus was having his coffee at the round table in Sweet's, and there was a crowd of us sitting there, four or five fishmongers and some of the shellfish gang, and Charlie came running up the stairs and asked Gus a question about a bill of lading, and Gus hauled off and shied a plate at him. 'Get out of here, you embezzler!' he said. 'When I want you,' he said, 'I'll send for you.' Right before everybody.

"Another thing about Gus, he tried to look poor. He tried to look like he didn't have a dime to his name. There's an old notion in Fulton Market: if you want to know a fishmonger's financial standing, don't bother Dun & Bradstreet, just look at him—if he looks like he's been rolling around in some gutter, his credit is good; if he's all dolled up, stay away from him. Gus Lowry carried that to an extreme. As soon as he got to his office in the morning, he'd hang his good suit in a locker and he'd put on a greasy old raggedy suit that was out at the elbow and patched in the seat and a coupla sizes too small for him to begin with, and he used a piece of rope he'd picked up somewhere for a belt, and he'd put on a pair of knee boots that always had fish scales sticking to them, and he'd slap on a hat that was so dirty you wouldn't carry bait in it. He wouldn't wear a necktie; some days he wouldn't even wear a shirt. He'd light a cigar, one of those cheap Italian cigars that they call rattails. He'd spit on the floor. Then he'd sit down at his desk, looking like something the cat dragged in, the King of the Bums, and he'd be ready for business.

"And if you had to do business with him, you just took it for granted you'd be skinned. He'd skin you alive and then he'd shake your hand and inquire about your family. Up on his office wall he had a sign which said, "KEEP SMILING", but *he* never smiled. And he had a sign which said, 'All that I am or hope to be I owe to my angel mother.' And he had poems about the flag stuck up there and friendship and only God can make a tree and let me live in a house by the side of the road and be a friend to man. He'd recite you one of those poems—you couldn't stop him—and he'd begin to cry. Gus liked to cry. He really enjoyed it. Next to doing something mean to somebody, he liked to cry. I went to his office many a time and found him sitting there with tears in his eyes. People said it was second childhood, but when it came to a dollar he wasn't in his second childhood. The strangest thing, when he was close to eighty he started going to see a woman that lived in a hotel up on Union Square, and everybody hoped and prayed she'd get him into a lot of trouble. She was an old busted-down actress of some kind, a singer. She'd sing and he'd cry; that was his idea of a high old time. He took me up there with him once to call on her. He wanted me to look her over and tell him what I thought of her, about like he'd ask my opinion on a consignment of jack shad. We hadn't hardly got in the door before she commenced to bang on the piano and sing. Oh, she was a noisy one. Gus asked her to sing 'I'll Take You Home Again, Kathleen,' and by the time she got to 'the ocean wild and wide' he was crying. He hung around her a year or more and then he quit. I guess maybe the poor old thing tried to borrow a dollar and seventy-five cents off him and it broke his heart.

"The summer of 1921, Gus took a trip to Havana, Cuba, doctor's orders, and one morning there came a cable he was dead. Bright's disease. As soon as the news got out it put everybody in a good humor. Some tried to act like they were sorry, but they couldn't keep a straight face, and pretty soon the fellows all over the market were slapping each other on the back and laughing and old Mr. Unger that kept the stall next to mine shouted out,

'Hooray for the Bright's disease!' Everybody was so glad for Charlie. Captain Oscar Doxsee had worked for Gus off and on for thirty years—he was captain of Gus's trawler—and I remember what he said when they told him Gus was dead. 'God is good,' he said. It was prohibition, but little Archie Ennis the scallop dealer had a quart of whiskey in his safe, bourbon, and he got it out and him and I and Captain Oscar and several others went over to Charlie's office to congratulate him. We figured a little celebration was in order. Well, what do you know? Charlie was sitting in there with his head in his hands. 'Ladies and gentlemen,' he said to us, 'this is the saddest day of my life.' *Oh, oh, oh*, we were disgusted! I've seen many and many a disgusting thing in my time, but that took the prize. 'Young man,' I thought to myself, 'the opinion your uncle had of you, he was right.'"

Mr. Bethea grunted. "Blood is thicker than water," he said.

"Yes," said Mrs. Treppel, "I guess that's one way of looking at it."

MR. CUSACK CAME SHUFFLING into the room. He'd finally made it.

"Well, look who's here," said Mrs. Treppel. "Old Drop-Dead Matty himself. Hello, Matty. Didn't you drop dead yet?"

Mr. Cusack disregarded her. "Happy birthday, Hugh," he said.

"Why, thank you, Matty," said Mr. Flood. "Matty, this is Tom Bethea. Tom's an embalmer."

"A what?" asked Mr. Cusack.

"I'm an embalmer," said Mr. Bethea. "I'm a trade embalmer."

Mr. Cusack stared at Mr. Bethea for a few moments. "How do you do, sir?" he said respectfully.

"Pleased to meet you," said Mr. Bethea. "I've heard Hugh speak of you. Sing us a song."

"Oh, no!" said Mr. Cusack. "I ain't in a singing mood."

"It was good of you to come, Matty," said Mr. Flood.

"Yes, it was," said Mr. Cusack. "I guess this is the last time I'll ever come. I can't stand those stairs no more. I've had some bad news. I was to the doctor for a checkup last Thursday and the way he diagnosed it, my heart's some better but I got the high blood pressure."

"I got the high blood pressure, too," said Mr. Fass.

"I got it, too," said Mr. Bethea. "Had it for years."

"Oh, for God's sake!" said Mrs. Treppel. She got to her feet and began to hop about the room. As she hopped, she sang a children's street song, a rope-skipping song—"Oh, I hurt, I hurt, I hurt all over. I got a toothache, a gum boil, a bellyache, a pain in my right side, a pain in my left side, a pimple on my nose."

"Shut up, Birdy, and behave yourself," said Mr. Flood. "Come over here, Matty, and sit down. What can I get you?"

"You can get me a glass of cold water," said Mr. Cusack. "I asked the doctor what about whiskey and he said it was the better part of wisdom to leave it alone. I haven't had a drink for six days. All I drink is water."

"If you was to drink a glass of water, Matty," said Mrs. Treppel, "it'd be weeks and weeks before your stomach got over the shock."

"Now look here, Birdy," Mr. Flood said, "don't

talk to Matty that way. I won't have it. The high blood pressure is a serious matter." He got up from his wicker rocking chair. "Here, Matty," he said, "take this chair. How do you feel tonight? Do you feel any worse than usual?"

"I feel irritable," said Mr. Cusack. He slapped the pillow in the chair a time or two and sat down. "It makes me irritable to see people drinking and enjoying themselves," he said. "If I can't drink it, I don't want *nobody* to drink it. I wish they'd bring prohibition back and I wish they'd enforce it. I got so I don't approve of whiskey."

Mr. Flood fixed himself a drink—half Scotch, half water, no ice—and went over and stood with an elbow on the mantelpiece. "I'm the same," he said. "I love it and I depend on it, but I don't approve of it. When I think of all the trouble it's caused me, I feel like I ought to pick some distillery at random and sue it for sixty-five million dollars. Still and all, there've been times if it hadn't been for whiskey, I don't know what would've become of me. It was either get drunk or throw the rope over the rafter. I've thought a lot about this matter over the years and I've come to the conclusion there's two ways of looking at whiskey—it gives and it takes away, it lifts you up and it knocks you down, it hurts and it heals, it kills and it resurrects—but whichever way you look at it, I'm glad I'm not the man that invented it. That's one thing I wouldn't want on my soul." He suddenly snapped his fingers. "He's the one!" he said. "I was lying in bed the other night, couldn't go to sleep, and I got to thinking about death and sin and hell and God, the way you do, and a question occurred to me, 'I wonder what man committed the worst sin in the entire history of the human race.' The man that invented whiskey, he's the one. When you stop and think of the mess and the monkey business and the fractured skulls and the commotion and the calamity and the stomach distress and the wife beating and the poor little children without any shoes and the howling and the hell raising *he's* been responsible for down through the centuries—why, good God A'mighty! Whoever he was, they've probably got him put away in a special brimstone pit, the deepest, red-hottest pit in hell, the one the preachers tell about, the one without any bottom." He took a long drink. "And then again," he continued, "just as likely, he might've gone to heaven."

"The man that invented cellophane," said Mr. Fass. "*He's* the one."

Mr. Cusack sighed. "I got to be careful what I eat, too," he said.

"Oh, Matty, Matty," said Mrs. Treppel, "please take a drink and cheer up."

"Leave me alone," said Mr. Cusack. He glanced at his wristwatch, and then he peered into every corner of the room. "Where's your radio, Hugh?" he asked. "There's a program coming on in five minutes I don't want to miss."

"I got no radio," said Mr. Flood.

Mr. Cusack looked disappointed. "You should get one," he said. "It'd do you a world of good. It'd be a comfort to you."

"It wouldn't be no comfort to me," said Mr. Flood. "I despise the radio. I can't endure it. All that idiotic talk and noise, it goes right through me; it jars my nerves. Son," he said to me, "you sit on the bed and let me have your chair. I'll open up some sea urchins and we'll have a snack."

He got out a fish knife he carries in a holster and began preparing the sea urchins. He had three or four dozen full-grown ones, the biggest of which was about the size of a man's clenched fist. Urchins are green, hemispherical marine animals. They are echinoderms; they are thickly covered with bristly prickles. They are gathered at low tide off rocky ledges on the southern Maine coast and shipped in bushel baskets. Fulton Market handles two hundred thousand pounds a summer, but they are rarely seen in restaurants. They are eaten in the home by Italians and Chinese; Italians call them *rizzi*, or sea eggs. Mr. Flood cut the tops off ten. He had trouble knifing through the leathery rinds and he muttered to himself as he worked. "Sorry damned knife," he muttered. "Stainless steel. They don't care if it's sharp or not, just so it's stainless, as if anybody gave a hoot about stains on a knife blade. I wish they'd leave knives alone, quit improving them. Look at it. Shiny. Stainless. Plastic handle. Only one thing wrong with it. It won't cut." Each urchin had a pocket of orange roe, from two to five tablespoonfuls. Mr. Flood spooned the roe out and spread it on slices of bread. Urchins are inexpensive, around fifty cents a dozen, but in Mr. Flood's opinion their roe is superior to caviar. He sprinkled lemon juice on the roe. Then he fixed six plates. On each he placed three open-faced roe sandwiches, a slice of eel, a herring, and a mound of pickled mussels. Mr. Fass refused his plate. "Drinking makes me hungry," he said, "but it don't make me that hungry."

ALL THE TIME MR. FLOOD had been preparing the urchins, Mr. Cusack had been staring at Mr. Bethea. Finally he spoke up. "I hope you won't think I'm prying into your affairs, Mr. Bethea," he said, "but there's two questions I'd like to ask you."

Mr. Bethea stopped eating for a moment. "It'll be a privilege to answer them, Mr. Cusack," he said, "if they ain't too personal."

"What I was wondering about is your line of work," Mr. Cusack said. "How in the world does a man ever come to take up that particular line of work?"

"Well, I tell you," said Mr. Bethea, "most of the embalmers of my generation started out as something else. Some were barbers and some were carpenters. I was a carpenter myself, a carpenter and cabinetmaker, and back in 1908 I took a job with Cantrell Brothers & Bishop, on Little West Twelfth Street. That was a coffin factory—what *we* call a casket factory. I built high-quality caskets for a year and a half, and you know how it is—an up-and-coming young man, you want to make something out of yourself. Every casket factory has a staff of embalmers, and I kept my eyes open when our staff was working and I asked questions and naturally I was handy with tools and the upshot was, I became an embalmer. I'm a trade embalmer, a free lance. We're the aristocrats of the trade—that is, the profession. All the overhead we have is a telephone. There's a multitude of undertaking parlors, little neighborhood affairs, that don't get enough cases to employ a steady embalmer. They just have a parlor with a desk and a pot of palms and a statue of an angel and a casket catalogue. Oh, some will have a sample casket or two on the premises. And there's seven or eight of these parlors, when they get a case, they telephone me. Wherever I go, I have to leave a number where I can be reached. And I get on the subway and I go and attend to the case and I collect my seventeen dollars—we got a union and that's the union rate—and I go on home. That's the end of the matter. I don't have to console the bereaved and I don't have to listen to the weeping and the wailing and I don't have to fuss with the floral offerings. Of course, these days, like everybody else, embalmers go to college. I went to college myself some years back, just to brush up on the latest scientific advances. There's two big colleges, the American Academy of Embalming and Mortuary Research on Lexington Avenue and the New York School of Embalming and Restorative Art on Fourth Avenue. They're the Harvard and the Yale of the embalming world. The past few years women have been flocking into the profession. You take the American Academy—a third of their students are women. I don't know. I may be old-timey, but the way I look at it, I just wouldn't have no confidence in a lady embalmer." He paused and glanced at Mrs. Treppel. "Present company excepted," he said.

Mrs. Treppel snorted. "If she puts her mind to it and works hard," she said, "I bet a woman can embalm as good as a man."

"I didn't mean to be rude," said Mr. Bethea. He

took the Scotch bottle by the neck and poured a big gollop in his glass. "I'm a disappointed man, Mr. Cusack," he continued. "If I had it to do all over again, I don't know as I'd choose embalming as my life's work. You don't get the respect that's due you. A doctor gets respect, a dentist gets respect, a veterinarian gets respect, but the average man, if he's introduced to an embalmer, he giggles or he shudders, one or the other. Some of my brother embalmers don't like to tell their profession to strangers. They're close-mouthed. They keep to themselves. Not me. Deep down inside, I'm proud of my profession. I carry a kit, a satchel, my professional satchel, and it's always been my dream to have my name printed on it. I can just see it—'THOMAS FOSTER BETHEA, LICENSED EMBALMER.' But I can't do it. If I got on the subway, the people would edge away. I'd have the whole car to myself. The public don't like to be reminded of death. It's going on all around them—like the fellow said, it looks like it's here to stay—but they want to keep it hid. We have to work like a thief in the night. I daresay there's not a one of you that's ever seen a deceased moved out of a New York apartment house or hotel. No, and you never will. We got ways." He smiled. "Oh, well," he said, "no matter how the public feels about embalmers, in the end some embalmer gets them all."

"You needn't be so happy about it," said Mr. Flood. "In the end, some embalmer's going to get you, too."

"That's the truth," said Mr. Bethea. He sighed. "It's a peculiar thing. I'm a veteran in my line. If you took all the deceased I've attended to and stood them shoulder to shoulder, they'd make a picket fence from here to Pittsburgh, both sides of the road. With all that in back of me, you'd think I wouldn't mind death. Oh, but I do! Every time I think about it in connection with myself, I tremble all over. What was that other question you wanted to ask, Mr. Cusack?"

"I wanted to ask, do you believe in a reward beyond the grave," said Mr. Cusack. "By that, I mean heaven or hell."

"No, sir," said Mr. Bethea, "I can't say that I do."

"Well, then," said Mr. Flood, "what makes you go to church so steady? You're there every Sunday in the year, Sunday school *and* sermon."

"Hugh," said Mr. Bethea, "it don't pay to be too cock-sure."

THE TURN OF THE CONVERSATION made me restless and I went over and sat on the window sill, with my plate in my lap, and looked out over the rooftops of the market. It was a full-moon night. There was a wind from the harbor and it blew the heady, blood-quickening, sensual smell of the market into the room. The Fulton Market smell is a commingling of smells. I tried to take it apart. I could distinguish the reek of the ancient fish and oyster houses, and the exhalations of the harbor. And I could distinguish the smell of tar, a smell that came from an attic on South Street, the net loft of a fishing-boat supply house, where trawler nets that have been dipped in tar vats are hung beside open windows to drain and dry. And I could distinguish the oak-woody smell of smoke from the stack of a loft on Beekman Street in which finnan haddies are cured; the furnace of this loft burns white-oak and hickory shavings and sawdust. And tangled in these smells were still other smells—the acrid smoke from the stacks of the row of coffee-roasting plants on Front Street, and the pungent smoke from the stack of the Purity Spice Mill on Dover Street, and the smell of rawhides from The Swamp, the tannery district, which adjoins the market on the north. Mr. Cusack came over and took a look out the window. He returned immediately to his chair.

"I'm thankful to God I'm not an officer walking the streets tonight," he said.

"Why's that, Matty?" asked Mr. Flood.

"It's a full-moon night," said Mr. Cusack. "There'll be peculiar things happening all over town. It's well known in the Police Department that a full-moon night stirs up trouble. It stirs up people's blood and brings out all the meanness and craziness in them, and it creates all manner of problems for policemen. A man or woman who's ordinarily twenty-five per cent batty, when the moon is full they're one hundred per cent batty. A full moon has a pull to it. Look at the tide; the tide is highest on a full moon. The moon pulls people this way and that way. With some, it's a feeble pull; they don't hardly notice it. Others just can't resist; they don't know what's got hold of them. They act peculiar. They act like bashi-bazouks. They pick on their wives and they get drunk and they insult people twice their size and they do their best to get into serious trouble. They look at black and say it's white, and if you don't agree it's white they hit you on the head. In the Department, we call such people full-mooners. It's been my experience that they're particularly numerous among the Irish and the Scandinavians and the people who come up here from the South. On a full-moon night the saloons are like magnets. The full-mooners try to walk past them and they get drawn right in."

"That explains a lot to me," said Mr. Flood. "I must be a full-mooner. I've started home many a night with no intention in the world of stopping off. It was the last thing in my mind. And four A.M. would come, and there I'd be, holding on to some bar, and I wouldn't half know how I got there."

"Exactly," said Mr. Cusack. "Some full-mooners get drunk and some get delusions. The Department is well aware of this. There's a glassed-in booth down in the lobby of Headquarters, the information booth. They have a calendar hanging in there, and they always have a red circle drawn around the date of the full moon. That's to remind the officer on duty what's ahead of him. I had an accident when I was in the Department, broke my leg, and I was a year and a half convalescing, and most of that time they had me on night duty in the information booth. And every full-moon night, I had visitors from all over. The full-mooners'd come trooping in. They'd step up and ask to see the Commissioner; nobody else would do. There was one who always came at midnight; he never missed. He'd ask for the Commissioner and I'd say, 'Lean over, sir, and whisper it to me. You can trust me.' And he'd lean over and whisper, 'They're after me!' And I'd get out my pad and pencil and ask for the details. And he'd talk on and on and on, and I'd take it all down. And I'd tell him, 'Rest assured the proper steps will be taken.' That'd satisfy him. He'd go away and I'd tear up whatever it was I took down and I'd throw it in the wastebasket." Mr. Cusack laughed. "Next full moon, he'd be back again."

"Mr. Cusack," said Mr. Bethea, "I recall a talk I had some years ago with an old gentlemen who works for one of the big cemeteries in Brooklyn, a foreman gravedigger. He said that a grave dug around the time of the new moon, the dirt that comes out of it won't fill it up. It'll have a sunk-in look. Whereas, a grave dug around the time of the full moon, there'll be plenty of dirt left over; you can make a nice mound on top. Another fact he told me, he said that women's bosoms get bigger during the time of the full moon. Did you know that?"

"No, I didn't, Mr. Bethea," said Mr. Cusack. "I'm glad you brought it up. While we're on the subject, I recall a case I was personally mixed-up in that might be of considerable interest to a man in your line."

"What was that?" asked Mr. Bethea.

"It happened in 1932, the year before I retired from the Department," said Mr. Cusack. "At the time I was attached to the First Precinct. One morning around four A.M. I was patrolling on South Street, proceeding east, and a radio car pulled up and the driver-officer informed me they were looking for two lads that stole an empty hearse. It seems this big black hearse had been parked in front of a garage on Third Avenue in the Sixties, the Nineteenth Precinct. The lads stole it and proceeded south on Third. Just ahead of them was a *Daily News* truck, delivering bundles of *Daily*

*News*es to newsstands. You know the way they operate; they pull up to a corner where there's a stand and heave a bundle out on the sidewalk. At that hour a good many stands haven't opened, and the bundle lies there until the man that runs the stand comes to work. The lads in the hearse conceived the idea of collecting these bundles. The hearse would pull up and one lad would leap out, grab a bundle, and heave it in the hearse. They went from stand to stand, doing this. Headquarters was soon getting calls from all over, people that saw them, and it was put on the police radio. The hearse was last seen on lower Broadway, heading for the Battery. I told the driver-officer I hadn't observed no hearse, but I got on the running board and went along to help search the South Street docks. We hadn't gone three blocks before we ran into them. They had the hearse backed up to the river, right beside the Porto Rico Line dock, and they were heaving the bundles of *Daily News*es in the water."

"That was the right place for them," said Mr. Flood.

At this moment, Mr. Trein, the manager of the Hartford, began to shout up the stairwell. "Is Mr. T.

F. Bethea up there?" he shouted.

Mr. Bethea went to the door. "That's me," he said.

"You're wanted on the telephone," said Mr. Trein.

"I'll be right down," said Mr. Bethea. Then he turned to Mr. Cusack. "Please go right ahead, Mr. Cusack," he said. "They'll hold on."

"I jumped off the running board of the radio car," continued Mr. Cusack, "and began to interrogate the lads. 'What are you lads doing?' I asked. One of them, the littlest, heaved another bundle in the drink, and he said to me, 'We're having some fun. What's it to you?' I asked them didn't they like newspapers, and they said they liked them all right. So I asked them what in hell was they heaving them bundles in the water for. They said they be damned if they knew. I asked was they drunk, and they said they wasn't. Maybe a beer or two. I asked was they narcotic addicts, and they said they wasn't. So I turned to the driver-officer, and I said, 'It looks to me they're Reds, or I.W.W.s, or Black Hands. All those radicals,' I said, 'are opposed to newspapers, the free press, and all like that.' And the driver-officer said to me, 'You sure are a thick one.' He jerked his thumb upwards, and I looked up and there was a full moon up there. It was as round as a basketball, and it was so full it was brimming over. It was very embarrassing. I just wasn't thinking. I should've known all along that those lads were full-mooners." —*(1945)*